Dear Reader,

This month, there's plenty to be thankful for—but romance should always be at the top of the list! And we have four dazzling new romances from Bouquet to offer!

What could be more romantic than a chance meeting? In Lori Handeland's **When You Wish,** a massage therapist couldn't be more surprised when the sexy man who walks into her office turns out to be an infuriatingly logical doctor—with a smile that melts her heart. And in **Her Best Man,** beloved author Lisa Plumley offers us the story of an impetuous heiress trying to do a simple favor for her best friend—and hijacking the wrong man! Unless he's right for her, of course. . . .

When love takes you by surprise, there's only one thing to do—fall for it! In Cheryl Holt's **Mountain Dreams,** a sensible businesswoman does just that—when she meets a legendary ladies' man who just might be ready to fall in love, too. Finally, Adrienne Basso proves that when a financial analyst agrees to masquerade as her boss's date for the weekend, neither one of them anticipates **A Night To Remember.**

Enjoy!

Kate Duffy
Editorial Director

ROMANCE

"DID YOU EVER WISH ON A STAR?"

Grace certainly changed subjects at the speed of light. "No."

"Never?"

Star wishing had not been encouraged in his family. Wishing was for losers. Doers got the prize. "What would be the point?"

"When you wish, your dreams come true."

"Yeah, right."

"Don't you believe in anything, Dan?"

"I believe in science."

"That's all?"

He thought a moment. "Pretty much."

"Well, I'll do whatever I have to, to make my dreams come true."

In that way they were alike. He'd do whatever it took to make his dream come true. But Dan knew when you wished, you only wasted time. From the way Grace was gazing up at the star-studded night, explaining his view would only waste more time. So he let the argument go—and before he could think about what he was doing, he put his hands on her shoulders.

And when she turned in his arms and tilted her chin to look into his eyes, that perfect brow scrunched up and her mouth irresistibly puckered. He closed the small gap of space between them and took what he'd been wanting to take since he'd seen her only hours before. . . .

WHEN YOU WISH

Lori Handeland

ZEBRA BOOKS
Kensington Publishing Corp.

http://www.zebrabooks.com

For Peggy Hoffmann—
who said one thing and, suddenly, this book made sense.

One

Five words and his whole life changed.

"Your grant is being reevaluated."

Dr. Daniel Chadwick stood in his laboratory, suddenly quite clear on why "killing the messenger" had once been an accepted practice. Right now Dan wanted to throttle the little weasel who smiled so politely while ruining his life.

"Exactly what constitutes reevaluation?"

Perry Schumacher's lips and nose twitched. If he'd had whiskers on that nose he couldn't have looked more weasel-like. Poor unfortunate soul, but Dan had no sympathy left.

"Mrs. Cabilla wants to make certain she is serving her late husband's memory to the best of her ability. You know the particulars of the grant: one lump sum, per year, to the charity of her choice."

Dan's teeth ground together as they always did whenever someone referred to his work as a charity. He was a medical research scientist on the cusp of a breakthrough that would aid countless human beings. Mrs. Cabilla knew that. She was the only person who understood Dan's need to champion the underdog—even if it was an underdog disease.

He opened his mouth to argue, but Perry got there first. "Mrs. Cabilla is aware of your progress. But after five years of funding your studies, her faith is nearly gone. She is considering another charity."

"Which one?"

"Project Hope."

"Never heard of it."

"That's because it's new."

"What's it for?"

Perry rustled the papers on his clipboard, looked down his weaselly nose, and sniffed. "Providing security blankets to gravely ill children."

The room went so silent Dan could hear the drip of the faucet next to his worktable—the faucet he never got around to tightening because he was always too busy. To be honest, he never noticed how annoying the sound was while in the zone of discovery. And he was in the zone a lot.

Plop, plop, plop. Dan shook his head to make the sound stop echoing. Didn't help. He stared at Perry, blinking in hopes that the little man would disappear. Didn't work.

"Tell me you're kidding."

Perry settled his chin upon his tightly knotted tie. His glasses slid down his nose and perched precariously on the tip. "I never kid."

"I just bet you don't." Dan ran his fingers through his hair, wondering how it had gotten so long again. He'd just had his hair cut, what, last week? He glanced at his watch and frowned. Make that last month. When the work was going well, he had better things to worry about than his hair.

Yanking off his lab coat, Dan advanced on Perry. "Where can I find her?"

Perry must have seen something he did not like in Dan's eyes because he backed out of the way, holding the clipboard in front of his face as if to stop Dan's fist. Small people always reacted that way when Dan was around, though he'd never touched anyone with violence in his life. Unfortunately, or fortunately, depending upon how one looked at it, Dan was huge—six-feet-five-inches, 230-pounds huge. Whenever anyone looked at him, they saw football player or All-Star wrestler, despite the M.D. behind his name and an IQ that could rival his weight.

"F-find who?" Perry stuttered.

"Mrs. Cabilla. I want to talk to her."

"She's unavailable."

Dan took another step toward Perry. "She'll be available for me."

Perry retreated some more, and his back came up against the wall. He lowered the clipboard an inch, and his tiny black eyes peered over the top. Weasel, no doubt about it. "No," he said. "She won't."

Dan resisted the urge to grab the clipboard and toss it over his shoulder. Such behavior might give Perry heart failure, and that Dan didn't want. At least not until Perry told him where he could find Mrs. Cabilla.

He inched closer, until he came toe to toe with Mrs. Cabilla's emissary. "Where?" he repeated.

"I can tell you, but it won't do you any good."

"Why not?"

Amazingly, Perry smiled. Dan frowned. If Perry

was happy, Dan would not be. Over the last five years he and Perry had never gotten on, probably because of the height thing. Being six feet five inches was a disadvantage, but try telling that to a man who was a foot shorter.

"Because she went to the Andes."

"A candy factory?"

Perry snorted and lowered the clipboard completely. "Do you ever look past your little world?"

"What for?"

"There is an amazingly huge universe beyond Northern Wisconsin."

Dan shrugged. "All I need is right here with me."

"Enjoy it while you can." Perry slid toward the door.

Dan put his hand against the wall, between Perry and escape. "Where?"

"The Andes mountains, Doctor. In Peru."

"Peru? What does Mrs. Cabilla want in Peru?"

"Yarn."

"Excuse me? I thought you said yarn."

"Nothing wrong with your hearing." Perry ducked beneath Dan's arm and opened the door. "Mrs. Cabilla has become quite taken with knitting for stress relief. Seems to work and she's very good at it. She wanted a special kind of yarn made from a sheep that wanders the Andes mountains."

"So she went to get it herself?" Dan couldn't quite believe what he was hearing.

"She has the money and the time. Why not?"

"Wait just one minute. Mrs. Cabilla has become a knitting freak, and she's considering giving my money to a foundation that provides blankets for kids?"

"No moss on your brain, Doc. And it's not *your* money. It's Mrs. Cabilla's money."

Dan flushed. "Of course it is. Who runs Project Hope?"

"Wouldn't you just like to know?" Perry slammed the door, and Dan heard him scurry off toward his car. After that parting shot, Dan wouldn't have been surprised if Perry had stuck out his tongue before fleeing. The man really didn't like him at all, which was fine with Dan.

"Knitting," Dan murmured. "Yarn. Sheep. Peru, for crying out loud."

Mrs. Cabilla had gone off her rocker. That was as plain as the day was new. But what could he do about it? That was the question.

Five years ago, at the ripe age of twenty-six, Dan had finished his studies and dedicated his life to science. Science was something he understood. What he could touch was real. What he could see was true. What he could discover was worth his life and more. He had finally found something he was good at, and since he was good at precious little, according to his family, Dan took what he had and ran with it.

He wasn't going to let some New Age, hip-hop charity take everything he'd worked so hard to achieve, right when he was about to achieve everything.

Dan grabbed the phone and punched in the number for directory information. "A new listing," he said when the operator came on the line. "Project Hope."

Northern Wisconsin was a land of contrasts. On

one hand, spacious and deserted: acres upon acres of trees and wildlife—a sportsman's paradise. Then right up a county highway would appear a tourist town—Minoqua, Eagle River, Bayfield—where there were shops and coffee houses, restaurants and lodges.

In the summer, the streets teemed with people wearing shorts and sunglasses. Winter brought a different crowd with snowmobile suits and boots, ski jackets and jaunty hats. It was into one of these towns, packed with summer shoppers, that Dan drove in search of Project Hope.

Lake Illusion, the town, sat along Lake Superior. Lake Illusion, the lake, was at the outskirts of the town, a perfect northwoods setting for Mrs. Cabilla's home. Dan's lab was housed in an abandoned Boy Scout camp on the opposite side of the same lake.

He squinted against the midafternoon sun. The address he'd received when he'd called the number for Project Hope was located on a quieter side street, away from the usual hustle and bustle on Lake Illusion's main drag. Plenty of parking down this street, as there were no pottery shops, Native American jewelry stores, or crystal havens—all tourist magnets. Dan parked his pickup truck at the curb in front of a large Victorian home, got out, then glanced at the paper in his hand.

Three hundred thirty-six. Odd, the place didn't look like an office but rather a residence. Dan frowned as he walked up the sidewalk. No sign at the front proclaiming the offices of Project Hope, just a wind chime hanging on the porch, swaying in the heated breeze and chiming a haunted tune.

The front door stood open, allowing him to see into the foyer through the screen door. Inside sat a respectable, little old lady behind an antique desk. Perhaps this was a bed-and-breakfast. If so, the woman would probably know where he could find Project Hope.

Dan opened the screen door and a bell rang. The woman, who'd been focused upon something in her lap, looked up and smiled a welcome. Now that he was closer, he saw she wasn't as respectable as he'd thought, nor as old. Her hair, a pale enough blond to look white, was drawn into a ponytail at her neck and reached all the way to the seat of her chair. Her eyes were the most extraordinary shade of russet-brown that Dan had ever seen and sparkled like polished stones. She wore dark red lipstick and Indian earrings that brushed the shoulders of her peasant blouse.

"Hello," he began.

She straightened and put a jumble of cloth onto the desk. "Come on in. Do you have an appointment?"

Dan moved close enough to see that the cloth she'd held in her lap was a quilt block. He remembered Perry's words about security blankets and frowned. Maybe he *was* in the right place after all.

"I'm looking for Project Hope—"

"You've found us. And you are?"

"Dr. Chadwick."

"Doctor! How lovely." She pressed her hands together as if in prayer and beamed at him over the tips of her fingers. "My ear has been bothering me ever since I went parasailing last week. Do you think it was the altitude? Or maybe I shouldn't have gone into the water at such a high speed."

She continued to look at him as if he could help her. Dan had never actually practiced medicine on people. Sure, he'd had to deal with them in school, but he'd never been any good at it. If he hadn't planned to go into research from the beginning, he would have once he realized how incredibly inept he was in the face of pain and emotion. He shouldn't be surprised, considering his parents. But that was neither here nor there.

"Doctor?"

"Uh, yes, well, I'm not sure." He tried to get past the image of this woman flying through the air with the greatest of ease. "I'm not an ear man, you see."

"A rear man, you say?"

Her ear must really be bothering her. "No," Dan said louder and clearer. "I'm not an ear man."

"Ah, what kind of man are you then? A leg man?"

Dan blushed, one of the embarrassments of being blond and fair-skinned. The woman laughed, delighted, and he blushed darker, his skin on fire all the way up to his forehead.

"You'll want to talk to Grace," she said, letting him off the hook.

"I will?"

"She's the brains behind Project Hope. It's been her baby, from the start."

"Yes, she'd be the one I want to talk to."

"She's between appointments." The woman waved toward a long hallway leading out of the foyer. "Go on down, second door on the left."

"Thank you." Dan followed the flip of her finger-
nails, painted the same garnet-red as her lips.

As he passed from the foyer into the house proper,
flute music played in the distance. The haunting mel-
ody drew him forward. As he neared the second door
on the left he caught the scent of apple pie and cinnamon. His stomach growled. Damn, he'd forgotten
to eat again. Professional hazard.

Clearing his throat, Dan opened the door to what
he thought was the mystery woman's office and
stepped inside.

It wasn't an office.

The scent of apples must have come from the
dozen or so candles that wavered in an unknown
breeze. His stomach contracted, and he felt dizzy
for a moment. A man of his size really had no
business forgetting to eat.

The only light came from the candles, giving the
room a moody glow. He'd stepped into another
world, and while Dan wasn't very comfortable in the
usual one, this one made him downright nervous.
He almost fled; then she appeared from behind the
Oriental screen.

Lithe and long, her black hair drifted past her
shoulders—loose, free, lovely. Her head tilted down
as she belted a red scarf about her slender waist. Her
legs, tanned and perfect, played hide-and-seek beneath the thigh-high slit in the flowing white skirt of
her dress. Dan swallowed and his eyes followed the
long, naked expanse of her calf toward her bare feet.

Excellent feet. Long and slim, with red polish on
the toes that matched the sash at her waist. He'd

seen painted toenails before; he wasn't a saint. But these, well. . . . He coughed.

Her head went up like a doe startled at the edge of the forest; her brown eyes searched the shadows. Dan couldn't speak; he stood there staring, trying to take in every nuance of her face.

His scientific mind began to catalog all he observed. Exotic, with high cheekbones, a strong nose, and supple, smooth, tanned flesh. Black lashes and brows, auburn lips, no makeup. The most gorgeous woman he'd ever seen.

"Are you here for me?" she asked.

Oh, yeah, his mind leered in a very unscientific manner. Dan just stood at the door and stared like a fool.

"Sir?" He nodded because he could not speak. "All right. I guess there's time for one more." She reached behind the screen and pulled out a bright white sheet. The contrast of the crisp, cool cotton in her tanned, slim hand made him think of autumn turned to winter, leaves beneath the snow, apple pies cooling at Christmas. He had lost what remained of his mind.

She tossed the sheet at him, and he caught it before the material slapped him in the face. "Everything off," she said. "On the table. Sheet goes over you both."

Before Dan could fathom what he'd just been told, she slipped out the door and left him alone.

"What the hell?" he muttered, staring at the cushioned table in the middle of the room. Candles, cushioned table, everything off? Dan clenched the sheet. He'd stumbled into the red-light district of Lake Illusion! He hadn't even known there was one.

But the parasailing lady had said Project Hope resided here. Did Grace of the great legs and even greater face have a dual life? Prostitute by day, charity maven by night. Or the other way around?

Dan moved across the room and looked behind the screen. More sparkling white sheets, several towels, and bottles of many colors. He picked one up.

Self-heating body oil.

"Uh-oh." Dan put the bottle of golden oil back where he'd found it.

He should get out of here as fast as he could. Call Grace, whatever her name was, and settle everything on the phone. But his entire life hung in the balance, and so did the good name of the Cabilla Grant. Mrs. Cabilla couldn't know she was planning to give many, many dollars to a house of ill repute, however deserving their charity program was. Dan wasn't a prude, but he needed that money.

What if he did take everything off and got on the table? His body responded to that image in a predictable manner. But only because he'd been alone for a long, long time. Medical research scientists on the cusp of discovery did not have time for sex or love. That was the only reason he couldn't seem to stop thinking of her incredible face, silky black hair, and long-fingered, clever hands.

"Damn," Dan muttered and began to undress. This was probably the biggest mistake of his life, but he needed to find out just what was going on at 336 Elm Street if he was going to tattle to Mrs. Cabilla. He wasn't proud of himself, but he was desperate. He'd stop things before they went too far. He would.

When the door opened again, Dan lay face down

on the table, the sheet modestly covering him from waist to ankle. Keeping his eyes closed, he waited to find out what Grace would say next.

She didn't speak; instead she moved about, then stopped at the table. Hands touched his shoulders, kneading the tense muscles, pushing at the knots of stress that made it hard for him to sleep at night, then slid over his skin, silky smooth. The oil, he recalled, and let out a sigh of pleasure.

She had large hands. Strong, too—amazingly so. Dan was a big man, and he worked out daily—otherwise he found his mind became as atrophied as his muscles, but Grace pushed at those muscles and dug into his spine. By the time she reached his lower back, he'd gone limp.

"Mmm," he murmured. "This is amazing. Does it cost extra?"

"Extra? What means extra?"

All the tension that had flowed from Dan's body came back with painful force as a heavily accented, male voice thundered from above.

Dan flipped onto his back and stared at the huge, blond monster in the bulging white T-shirt. "Who are you?"

Sniff. "I am Olaf."

"Where's Grace?"

"Gracie does not massage men. It is inappropriate, she says."

"Huh?"

"Not illegal. No. But she does not feel right. And a big man like you . . ." Olaf shrugged. "She could not do a good job. Her hands are strong for a woman, but they are not the hands of Olaf."

"Whoa, this is a massage parlor?"

"What did you think?"

Dan looked at the size of Olaf and remembered how his voice had caressed the word "Gracie." He wasn't going to tell the man he'd thought Grace was offering more than the house special. That would be the quickest way to get his nose broken. He probably deserved it, but he'd rather pass on physical violence while naked. Dan started to get up.

Olaf shoved him back down. "Turn over. Silence. I do not like to talk while I work."

"There's been a misunderstanding. I came here to talk about Project Hope."

"If you wish to talk of Hope, why do you lay on this table? Naked. Why do you ask for Gracie?" Olaf's fingers, which had been on Dan's shoulders, suddenly dug into the sensitive cavity beneath his collarbone.

"Ouch." Dan jumped from the table before Olaf could take off his head. He clutched the sheet around his middle and put the table between him and the other man. Dan had never before felt threatened by another human being, but all of a sudden he understood why most people got out of his way. Dan very much wanted to get out of Olaf's way right now. "I said this was a misunderstanding."

"I know what kind of misunderstanding you have. This is why Gracie has me." He thumped a hamlike hand against his chest. "Olaf is to make sure no one touches Gracie with inappropriateness. People think because we massage we also do other things. But we do not!"

"Of course not," Dan agreed. Damn, he wished

he had his clothes. Olaf's face was getting redder by the second.

"Americans have no understanding of the ways of the body. All is medicine, science. What they can see and touch." Then Olaf actually hissed. Dan had never heard a man hiss; it was quite effective. "You do not understand that what you do not see is more powerful than anything of this earth."

Dan had never been able to understand what he could not see and touch, but he wouldn't argue with Olaf if the masseur told him moon men had taken over every cheese factory in Wisconsin. Instead he nodded and slid toward the screen.

Olaf blocked his way. Dan looked up into Olaf's furious face. The guy had to be seven feet of pure muscle. Dan was going to have to talk his way out of this one, but talking had never been one of his better talents—especially talking while seminude.

"Listen, Olaf, I made a mistake. I apologize. I'll pay you for your time. But I really need to talk to Grace."

"No." Olaf shook his finger in Dan's face. "There will be no talking to Gracie for a bad man like you." Then Olaf reached out and yanked the sheet from Dan's grasping fingers.

Three things happened at almost the same time. Dan made a grab for the sheet, Olaf tossed it over his shoulder with an evil grin, and Grace walked in the door.

All three of them stood frozen for a moment. Then Dan dove for the screen, Olaf started laughing, and Grace asked, "Are you Dr. Chadwick?"

Two

By the time Grace had calmed Olaf and sent him on his way, the doctor was dressed. Even so, she couldn't forget the sight of him standing naked as a jaybird.

He'd been magnificent, standing there with the candlelight flickering across his body—big and strong, with curves and dips and muscles in all the right places.

Grace had a vision of what her ancestors had been subjected to centuries ago. If you put a sword in one hand, a shield in the other, and some kind of fur over his shoulder, you'd have a Viking invader climbing from his boat onto the shores of the New World. Now Grace had never been much for Vikings—being a Green Bay Packer fan herself—but wow, this one was something to see.

"You're the administrator of Project Hope?"

Chadwick's voice startled Grace from her mini fantasy. He stepped through the doorway and joined her in the hall. Nodding, she reached past him to close the door of her massage room. Her arm brushed his belly, and a tingling sensation ran all the way to her neck. His stuffy white shirt did nothing to stop the image of supple, smooth skin stretched over well-defined stomach muscles from appearing in her mind.

He hadn't tied his tie, leaving the strip of bland, navy blue material looped around his neck. The starched shirt gaped open, and when he swallowed, the slide of his throat muscles made her shiver. How was she going to talk business with this man if every time she looked at him she remembered what he looked like naked?

"Miss?"

Grace blinked. She'd been standing too close, staring at his throat. Stepping back, she glanced at his face. He stared at her with rapt attention as well, but his eyes focused on her lips.

Self-consciously she wiped her mouth, half afraid she had drool on her chin. His eyes, the color of a sky surrounding a full moon—dark, yet somehow blue—followed the movement. Then he muttered and turned away, dragging a large, blunt-fingered hand through hair the shade of sand and sun. For a doctor, he had awfully long hair.

"I'm sorry, Doctor, but I don't understand. If you came here to talk about my project why didn't you say so? You've gotten Olaf all excited. He thinks you're a . . ."

Grace let her voice trail off. Olaf's exact words were not fit for repeating, being in Norwegian and roughly translatable as "whoremaster."

Those solemn eyes returned to hers. "A what?"

"Never mind. I think there's been a huge misunderstanding."

"Yes," he agreed quickly. "I apologize, Miss . . .

I'm afraid I don't know your full name. Just Grace, as the woman in the front called you, or Gracie." He shrugged.

"My last name is Lighthorse, but I think we've gone past Miss and Doctor, don't you?"

She couldn't be sure, but she thought he blushed. You had to like a guy who topped six feet and could still blush.

"Lighthorse?" he asked. "You're Native American?"

Obviously he hadn't looked at her as closely as she'd thought he'd been looking. "Aren't we all?"

"Excuse me?"

"You were born in this country; so was I. Native."

"I didn't mean to offend."

"You didn't." She should be used to questions by now. She'd lived in the north woods all of her twenty-eight years, yet she never ceased to be amazed that people were surprised to find Indians there. "I'm Ojibway." Her voice became brisk. "Lac du Flambeau. But if you just call me Grace, I won't call you white guy."

That got a smile out of him. "Fine with me," he agreed, and held out his hand. "I'm Dan."

Dan didn't look like he smiled often, but when he managed, the effect was devastating. Grace folded her lips together. No drooling, even in her imagination.

She shook his hand, refusing to acknowledge the flicker of awareness that continued to haunt her. He had calluses on those big hands, and they rubbed along her palm in an enticing way.

"I'd like to discuss Project Hope," he said. "Is there somewhere we can talk?"

"Yes. Certainly."

He tugged on his hand, and she let go with a grind of her teeth. She seemed to have developed a thing for big guys with rough hands.

Having a doctor come to speak with her about Project Hope made this a banner day. Grace had figured she would be fighting the medical profession tooth and nail for a long while. From what she'd seen so far, none of them had any vision. But Mrs. Cabilla's grant would help to gain respect for her dream. Money talked everywhere.

The two of them climbed the stairs to the second floor, which had once housed six bedrooms. The previous owner had knocked out walls, constructing a great room with a western window exposure. As Grace and Dan reached the top of the stairs, the chitter-chatter from the Jewels reached their ears, and Grace couldn't help but smile. She'd had the Jewels in her life, together or in various combinations, since the day she was born. She adored them, eccentricities and all.

After crossing the few short steps from the landing to the curved archway of the great room, Grace gazed at the familiar scene. Three elderly ladies could make quite a mess when given free reign with scissors, fabric, batting, and thread. They liked to work amidst clutter, and since they were geniuses, she let them.

"Aunt Em?" she called.

"Aunt Em?" Dan echoed. "As in Auntie Em, there's no place like home?"

Grace rolled her eyes. "No, as in Emerald. You met Garnet downstairs; the redhead is Ruby. My mother's sisters, known as 'The Jewels of Dublin.' "

"Ireland?"

"South Dakota."

Dan continued to contemplate the piles of fabric and batting, as well as the three tiny ladies who flitted among them. "I'm confused."

"Don't be. It's quite simple. My great-grandparents, on my mother's side, came from Ireland. They started a little town in the West. My grandparents had four daughters."

"The Jewels."

"Right.

"And your mother's name?

"Di."

"Diana?"

Grace snorted. The man had no imagination whatsoever. But what could she expect from a doctor? "Diamond."

"Your mother's name is Diamond Lighthorse?"

"Is that a problem?"

"Of course not. I just want to be clear before I meet her."

"You won't. She's no longer with us."

He turned his head and his sympathetic gaze met hers. "I'm sorry for your loss."

Doctor talk. She'd heard it all before. He couldn't help it. That's what he was trained to say, though the sympathy in his eyes seemed real. "She's not dead," Grace clarified. "She's just no longer with us."

"Oh. I see."

His voice said very clearly that he did not see at all, but Grace wasn't about to share private heartaches with a stranger—even though he wasn't quite a stranger anymore. Her mother had been unwilling to come back to Wisconsin. She'd preferred to stay in Minnesota, alone, when Grace and the Jewels went looking for a new home. Though Grace was happy to be in the land of her birth once again, she missed her mother, but at least she had Em and the others.

Grace called to her aunt, louder this time. The Jewels's hearing wasn't what it used to be. "Aunt Em!"

Her eldest aunt looked up, smiled, then picked her way across the room. The other two, occupied with choosing material from the stack of bolts near the far wall, merely raised a hand in hello and went back to arguing over the merits of rust over burnt-orange, their heads bobbing with the force of their customary arguments. The bickering was a sister thing Grace had never understood, since she'd never had a sister. The continuous arguing over nothing had bothered her at first until she realized they liked to argue. It was the way they showed their affection.

"Grace!" The sun through the windows sparkled across Em's recently retouched black roots. "All done for the day?"

"Yes, ma'am."

Em's green gaze wandered all the way up Dan's long body, then all the way down. Female appreciation filled her eyes. "And you saved one for me? Thoughtful girl."

Grace glanced at Dan to see if he was blushing again. He was. His mouth opened, then shut. He shuffled his big feet, then held out a huge hand, enveloping Em's fingers with his own. "Ma'am, it's a pleasure."

Amazingly, Em blushed, too. She'd buried five husbands and was on the lookout for number six. The spark in her eye made Grace think her aunt toyed with the idea of a younger man this time around.

"Aunt Em, Dr. Chadwick is here about Project Hope."

"Doctor? How interesting." She pulled her hand from his, then flicked her wrist up and down.

Dan glanced at Grace, a polite half-smile at war with the confusion filling his eyes. He looked back at Em, who was still flapping her wrist like an out-raged puppeteer. "It hurts when I do this," she said.

"Then don't do that?" The punchline came out with the lilt of a question, as if he didn't know that Em was asking him for advice. What kind of doctor wasn't used to being quizzed on aches and pains at every opportunity?

"Never mind," Grace told Em. "I stopped by to see how far you've gotten today."

After sending a curious glance in Dan's direction, Em dropped her hand. "We finished the crazy quilt, packed it up, and sent the box to FedEx with Olaf."

"Good. What are you starting now?"

"Wedding Ring, for the Macieweski wedding."

"I'll be back soon to help cut the pieces."

Em nodded, then patted Dan on the arm as if he were a lost little boy. "It's all right, sweetie. Sometimes I pretend to be Cleopatra, Queen of the Nile. No one minds."

She bustled off in a swish of multicolored skirts, and Dan stared after her, dumbstruck. "She thinks I'm pretending to be a doctor?"

"You have to admit, you don't act like one."

"I don't?" Now he not only looked like a lost boy, he sounded like one.

Grace shook her head. "And you definitely don't look like one."

He grunted, as if he'd heard that before, and no doubt he had. Grace berated herself for mentioning it. She of all people should know that it was best not to judge by appearance.

"What *do* I look like?" he asked.

Viking marauder, her mind whispered. *Romance novel cover model. All-Star wrestler.*

"Lumberjack," she blurted.

That made him smile again, and for a moment Grace just enjoyed the view. She really did like how he looked. For a woman who got looked at a lot, she should know better than to stare, but she couldn't seem to help herself.

The longer they gazed into each other's eyes, the harder it became to look away. His gaze dropped to her mouth and Grace caught her breath. For some insane reason, she thought he meant to kiss her. And for a lunatic second, she wanted him to.

Then Ruby's voice shattered the thick, charged silence. "He's a doctor! Maybe I can show him my corns."

Dan started and looked over his shoulder, his face

exhibiting an odd combination of alarm and morbid fascination.

"Come on!" Grace turned around and headed down the hall. Dan followed right on her heels.

The offices of Project Hope and Quilts to Order, the mail-order business of the Jewels, were housed in the only bedroom not ceded to the great room. Not much of an office—scratched-up desk, rotary phone, new answering machine, old kitchen chairs and a battered filing cabinet—but Project Hope was still a baby. If the grant came through, Grace would have to use some of the money to assemble a real office and maybe hire a real secretary. The Jewels should really devote all their time to making the quilts they were becoming famous for.

Grace took the chair behind the desk, and Dan took the one on the other side. The metal creaked beneath his weight and they both winced.

"Now, Doctor—" He raised an eyebrow. "I mean, Dan, you'd like more information about Project Hope? You wish to make a donation? Money? Blankets? Time? Or maybe you can help me distribute the blankets. I have to tell you, I don't have any hospital contacts yet. I'm still waiting for final word on a grant."

"That's why I'm here."

It was Grace's turn to be confused. "The grant? You're from Mrs. Cabilla?"

"No, or at least not in the way you think." He sighed, then stood and paced the tight confines of the office. His size made the movement ridiculous, and he stopped with a growl of impatience, placing both hands in the center of Grace's desk and looming over her. "I'm the man who's spent five years trying to discover a way to prevent paronychial infections. If Mrs. Cabilla gives the money to Project Hope, everything I've done thus far will be worth nothing."

Grace stood. She wasn't going to let him loom over her. She knew that tactic for the intimidation ploy it was. Though why he wanted to intimidate her she had no idea. "I don't understand."

"I'm sure you don't. That's why I came to talk to you. I want you to withdraw your grant application. If you don't, thousands, perhaps millions, of people will suffer."

She'd ordered him out of her office, followed him down the stairs and shooed him out the front door. Good riddance! She wasn't letting Dr. Daniel Chadwick into her home again. The nerve of the man! Trying to take her money. Trying to kill her dream. Trying to imply that Project Hope was a joke and his research oh, so very important.

But paronychial infections did sound serious— and painful.

"Arrgh!" She slammed the door and stomped back up the stairs. Luckily the Jewels were just deaf enough not to notice her grumbling and stamping, because she didn't want to talk to anyone right then. She wanted to stew and fume, then she'd call Mrs. Cabilla and settle this once and for all.

Grace was not going to let Dr. Dan make her feel unworthy. If his research was so great, people would be standing in line to give him money. He didn't need to take away the only chance she had to make a wish, a dream, and a promise, come true.

Grace crossed to the window overlooking the street and peeked around the curtain. He still stood next to his car, gazing at the house.

How could such a jerk be so cute? How could such a creep have such an incredible body? How could such a . . . a . . . a *stiff* pretend to be such a nice guy?

Dan's wide shoulders slumped and he shook his head. For a moment he looked so dejected, Grace felt kind of bad. Then she reminded herself who and what he was: the enemy of her dream.

"Grace?"

"Hmm?"

She continued to stare out the window as he got in his car and drove out of her life forever. Good riddance, she thought once more. So why did she feel so bereft?

Aunt Em joined her at the window, but there was nothing left to see except a distant Lake Illusion sparkling in the sheen of the late afternoon sun. "What did Dr. Magnificent want?"

Grace smiled. Em never changed. Men were her forte. "He was, wasn't he?"

"Magnificent? You bet your moccasins. If he hadn't been looking at you like the last cream puff on the dessert tray, I might have snapped him up. But even with my extensive know-how, I doubt I'd be able to seduce that man away from you."

"He won't be looking at me again, and I won't be looking at him."

"Did he go medical on you?" Em asked.

Em had no patience for those who didn't understand magic and mystery. Her grandmother had been a healer in Ireland and passed the knowledge of herbs and the like on to her eldest daughter, who in turn passed it on to her eldest daughter.

Em's second husband—or maybe it was her first—had been a doctor and forbade Em to use her "witchy brews on innocent people." When Em continued to heal those who asked for help, he'd burned her granny's book—and dropped dead the next day. Em's sisters always said he'd been cursed by the spirit of their grandmother. Em merely smiled and married number three. Or had it been number two?

"He wants me to give up Project Hope," Grace explained. "He's received the Cabilla Grant for the past five years, and he says he's near to curing some kind of infection."

"That's what they all say."

When Grace didn't answer, Em took her hand, and led Grace into the great room. "Come on in here and see what we've done on the Wedding Ring quilt."

Ruby and Garnet joined them, chattering all at once as they explained the nuances of color they had agreed upon while she was gone.

Their handmade quilts sold for nearly one thousand dollars apiece, as they were masterpieces of skill and beauty, and took a lot of time to make. Very few people made quilts the ancient way—with their hands, no machines—but the Jewels always had, always would. What the Jewels made selling the quilts, combined with their social security, kept them in Irish whiskey and their house.

As her aunts flitted about the room, gathering patterns, fabric, and the sharpest scissors, Grace reminded herself again why Project Hope was so important. She'd seen enough sick kids to know that sometimes there was nothing you could do but give them something to hold on to.

Grace reached into the pocket of her dress and pulled out the tiny scrap of peach flannel she carried with her wherever she went. She rubbed the soft fabric against her cheek, and for an instant she caught the scent of hope. This bit of blanket reminded Grace of principles she held close to her heart: peace, and love, and something to hold on to when the world dished out its worst.

If Daniel Chadwick wanted a fight, a fight he would get. Grace was not giving up Project Hope. She couldn't and still look at herself in the mirror each morning.

Three

The summons to the lake home of Mrs. Cabilla came before the sun set on Grace's anger. She should have known Chadwick would run to Mommy and tattle. He just hadn't seemed the type—more a face-to-face kind of guy. Why else had he come looking for her in the first place?

Grace had been to the mansion many times, as Mrs. Cabilla was a client. When Grace met Mrs. Cabilla she had been one stressed-out lady, her shoulder muscles wound so tightly the woman couldn't breathe. She had ended up in the ER with chest pains.

After having massage recommended by her therapist, Mrs. Cabilla tried Grace and became a believer. Grace also introduced her to the soothing hobby of handiwork. Because while the mind and the hands were focused upon a repetitive task, the never-ending wheel of problems melted away, at least for a little while.

Mrs. Cabilla took to knitting like a trout to a stream, and whenever her world got a bit too much for her, she made another afghan. There were quite a few afghans lying around the mansion, which was how Grace's concept for Project Hope came into their conversations.

Grace rang the bell next to the huge double doors at the front of the Cabilla lake home, then listened as the bing-bong, bing-bong, echoed through the house. The doorbell always made Grace feel kind of lonely. Such a big house for such a tiny woman.

Mrs. Cabilla and her husband had been inseparable during their forty-five years of marriage, and losing him six years ago had broken her heart. Having no children to remember him by, or to soothe her loneliness, she had thrown herself into administering the vast estate left by the man she adored. But Mrs. Cabilla hadn't a clue about money, which was where Perry Schumacher came in.

The man in question opened the door and stared down his long, thin nose at Grace. She couldn't figure out why he didn't like her; she'd done nothing but help Mrs. Cabilla. Maybe he thought she took advantage of the friendship in applying for the grant. But, as Mrs. Cabilla said, the money had to go to someone, why shouldn't it be used to make Grace's wish come true?

"Miss Lighthorse, right on time as usual. Please come in. Welcome."

The twist of his lips told her she wasn't welcome, but then she'd never been welcome when Perry was around. Her grandfather would have dubbed him "weasel spirit." Grace turned a surprised chuckle into a cough. Perry would not be amused. She doubted much amused Perry.

Grace experienced a twinge of unease. Maybe he felt the money should go to Dr. Chadwick. If Chadwick were indeed close to curing paronychial infection, whatever it was, wasn't that worth putting her dream on hold for a little while longer? *Should* she withdraw her application?

But would she ever find another foundation willing to take her seriously? If she gave up this chance, what she believed in with all her heart might never come to pass.

"Have a seat," Perry ordered.

"Where's Mrs. Cabilla?"

"Peru." Perry moved his glasses up the bridge of his nose so he could peer at her as if she were a bug on a pin. "Don't you remember?"

"Of course I remember. But why am I here if she's still there?"

"Conference call," he chimed as if announcing dinner.

"Now?"

"As soon as Dr. Deadly shows up."

"Who?"

"You know, the big guy."

From the sight of Perry's pruned lips, Grace figured he didn't care for Chadwick either. Interesting. Maybe Perry just didn't like anyone. That thought warmed Grace's heart. And here she'd thought he only looked down his long nose at her.

Bing-bong, bing-bong.

Grace caught her breath. Showdown at the OK Corral. Her palms began to sweat. Business situations had never been her strong point.

Perry scuttled off to get the door. From the echoing silence, the mansion on the lake must be deserted but for the three of them. No need for servants when the lady of the manor was away. Still, the place seemed kind of spooky with the shadows of an approaching summer evening spreading across the living room floor toward her feet.

This place *was* secluded, and Perry *was* kind of weird. What if the doorbell ringer was Perry's accomplice and not the incredible doctor?

"Accomplice?" Grace shook her head and stood, drifting to the floor-length window that overlooked Lake Illusion. "You are losing it, Grace."

What might Perry do? Kidnap her? Why? She was broke down to her last dollar, and the Jewels weren't in much better shape. There were other things Perry could have lured her here for, but she doubted he could work up the enthusiasm for any of them.

A male voice in the hallway made Grace relax. She'd only met him once, but she would recognize the deep, mellow tone of Daniel Chadwick's voice in the dark.

The dark? Grace put her hand to her head. She had to stop thinking about him in those terms. There would be no fraternizing with this enemy.

The two men appeared in the doorway, and the contrast between them made Grace's heart beat faster. Dan looked even larger next to Perry, less stuffy, because when compared to Schumacher, Prince Charles would look like a wild and crazy guy. Even without a comparison, Dan was downright handsome—to a woman who liked large, blond, Viking invaders.

When had she become that kind of woman? Grace glanced at her watch. About five hours ago, it seemed.

When Dan saw her he stopped in his tracks and Perry, staring at his clipboard, ran smack into the doctor's back, bouncing backward like a bumper car. His clipboard went flying; his papers scattered, and he wheeled his arms madly. Dan spun about, quick despite his size, and grabbed the smaller man before he fell.

"Hey, there," he said, as Perry found his feet. "You okay?"

Perry jerked his arm from Dan's hand quite rudely, sniffed, and bent to pick up his things. "Watch where you're going," he muttered.

Dan glanced at Grace and lifted an eyebrow. Grace fought not to smile, though she wanted to share a smile with Dan over Perry's obvious distaste for them both. But she feared if she softened even a little she would lose everything she'd fought so hard to get. Dan was the enemy. She had to remember that, even though she really wanted to forget.

"Hello, Doctor."

He raised his eyebrows at her frosty greeting, glanced at Perry, then shrugged, and stepped into the room. He held out his hand. "Miss Lighthorse, we meet again."

Remembering the odd sizzle that had occurred the last time he'd taken her hand, Grace hesitated. But she would not be as rude as Perry, so she let Dan take her hand in his.

Big mistake. His warmth soothed her chill. His large, strong hand enveloped her smaller, slimmer one. Her fingers were strong, from her work, but she could sense the power of this man within her hand. His calluses rasped along her palm, and the reminder of that imperfection made her wonder: Why would a research scientist have the hands of a day laborer?

Before she could ask, he pulled away. Grace looked into his face and found a scowl. He turned abruptly. "I'm surprised you went running to Mrs. Cabilla so quickly. You don't seem the type to tattle."

"Me?" Grace asked. "But I thought you—"

"Conference call!" Perry chimed from the doorway. As if on cue, the phone rang. He bustled into the room, ordering them about like a general. "Doctor, you sit here. Miss Lighthorse, here. Mrs. Cabilla is a busy, busy woman. So let's get this settled, shall we?"

Before either of them could agree, disagree, or spit in his eye, he pushed a button on a phone that sat upon the coffee table between them.

Mrs. Cabilla's voice filled the room. "Daniel?"

"Yes, ma'am."

"Grace?"

"Yes?"

"Perry?"

"Ma'am."

Grace waited for him to click his heels and bow like a tin soldier. She'd never understood Mrs. Cabilla's devotion to this abrasive man. He must have positive traits unseen by the human eye.

"You can go, Perry. Thank you."

"Yes, ma'am."

An actual smile tilted his too-thin lips, and a sly glint sparked in his eye. He knew something, and Grace had a feeling neither she nor Dan would like what was about to occur.

Before she could demand an explanation for this entire charade, Perry scuttled from the room, and Mrs. Cabilla began to speak. "I hear you two are tussling."

"Tussling?" Dan stared at the phone as if he could see Mrs. Cabilla in Peru if he only stared hard enough.

"Fighting over money is so . . . so . . . so *bourgeois.*"

"Only people with money to spare would think so," Grace replied.

Dan glanced at her as if he couldn't believe she'd speak so to Mrs. Cabilla, but she always had. Mrs. Cabilla liked it, probably because no else dared.

Mrs. Cabilla chuckled. "How true, Grace, how true. Still, I don't want you two squabbling over my darling Drew's legacy. That would demean everything he meant the grant to stand for."

"What do you suggest?"

"I'm going to leave that up to the two of you."

"Huh?" Grace and Dan said at exactly the same time.

"You are two intelligent young people. I adore you both. I agree that you each have equally legitimate pursuits for the Cabilla Grant."

"Can't we split it?" Grace asked.

"No," Dan answered. "The grant is for one charity . . ." His mouth puckered on the last word. "Per year. No divisions."

"True," Mrs. Cabilla said. "The two of you need to come to an understanding. I'm having a lovely time here in the mountains. Grace, you wouldn't believe what I'm learning. There is a man here, I guess you would call him a witch doctor." She giggled. "But he's so wise."

Dan moaned and put a hand over his face. Grace ignored him. "What kind of witch doctor?"

"I don't know, dear. All I know is I feel younger than I have since Drew died. We sit on the beach, and we talk, and we laugh, and he has given me a potion for my shoulder that makes me forget it ever hurt at all."

"Rum," Dan muttered. "Maybe tequila."

Grace shot him an annoyed glare, which he didn't see because he was still holding onto his head like he had a hangover. Dan was not helping matters. Though she'd been the one to lead Mrs. Cabilla away from a life of stress and pain and onto the path of rejuvenation and relaxation, and she was glad to hear joy in Mrs. Cabilla's voice for the first time ever, Grace still didn't like the smell of this.

"I'm going to stay awhile longer. One thing I've learned from *Abuelo* is the need to see all sides to a question. The only way to find the answer you seek is to listen to the voice of the universe."

"Mrs. Cabilla, what *are* you talking about?" Dan sounded as if he might be sick.

Grace could sympathize. Those not familiar with the mystical path were often unduly confused by it. Dr. Dan's head must feel ready to explode.

"This is what I propose—Grace will help you at the lab, Dan."

Dan stood up so fast Grace wondered if the blood loss from the movement would make him go down like a rock. The pale cast to his face made her get up, too. She wouldn't be able to stop him from falling, but she might keep his head from smacking on the marble tile, which would avoid a long trip to the ER for everyone.

Grace glanced about the room. At least she would have plenty of blankets to cover him and stave off shock. There must have been an afghan on the back of every chair and couch.

Dan took a deep breath, drawing Grace's attention away from the blankets and back to his face. His color looked better. "Mrs. Cabilla, I work alone."

Bah, bah, bah, bum—with nobody else, sang George Thoroughgood in Grace's mind. Of course the song was "I Drink Alone," but the concept was the same. When Dr. Dan worked alone, he obviously preferred to be by himself.

"Not anymore. There is an interesting theory down here, which roughly translates to walking a mile in another's shoes. I think both of you would benefit by such a walk. Grace, you need to understand the medical mind-set in order to work with the people who can give approval to Project Hope. You need to speak their language, or they'll never take you seriously."

Grace sighed. True enough. She'd been turned away countless times, seen as a fruitcake, nutcase, banana-brain and several other food groups. Because of how she looked, how she dressed, what she did, no one in the medical field would listen to her, despite the fact that her IQ was in the genius range. To them, if you were smart you were a doctor, or a lawyer, not a back-rubber.

"And, Dan, you seem to be stalled at the very cusp

of your discovery. I think being alone too much is clouding your vision. How can you visualize a cure, if all you see is what is right in front of you? If all you hear is your own heart beating? Listen to the music of the universe."

"Do you have any idea what she's talking about?" Dan asked.

"Unfortunately, yes. If you look too hard at something, you miss what's all around you."

"You've lost me."

Don't I wish, Grace thought. "Look at it this way," she said, "a cure is a theory that has been proven correct. A theory comes from nothing. Disease is caused by germs, cells, DNA. Things you can't see."

"Under a microscope I can see them just fine."

"Truth can't be found under a microscope."

"Since when?"

Mrs. Cabilla's chuckle made Grace realize she and the good doctor were nearly nose to nose. She stepped back and so did he.

"I think you two will have an interesting three weeks."

"Three weeks?" Dan's voice was incredulous.

"Yes, by then I'll either be home, or I'll call again, and I'll expect you two to have worked this out."

"I don't understand how—" Grace began.

Mrs. Cabilla ran roughshod over Grace's words. "If either one of you doesn't wish to play by my rules, I'll consider it a withdrawal of your grant application. Are we clear?"

Dan looked at Grace. Grace looked at Dan. They

scowled at each other, then turned to address the disembodied voice of Mrs. Cabilla.

"Crystal, ma'am."

Dan felt like he'd been turned inside out and back again. He was exhausted and at a complete loss. How had his world gotten so screwed up in the span of a single day?

Dan did not like change. Change made him nervous. Change was never good. He liked his life ordered. With order came security, and with security came peace. And only when Dan was at peace could he work with any sort of brilliance.

He and Grace stood in the living room long after Mrs. Cabilla wished them a cheery *"Adios!"*

"Well, Doctor, I guess we should discuss this development."

Dan turned from the window and his contemplation of the North Star shining over Lake Illusion. He looked into Grace's incredible face and wished he could despise her. Yet he couldn't help but be drawn to her and he didn't know why. Could it merely be her beauty and the mysterious, enticing scent that surrounded her, combined with the tiny problem of having had no sex for the last year? Was he really that shallow?

Could be. Probably was. Why else did he want to kiss her every time he saw her? He'd never felt that way before. Dan was a reasonable man. With reasonable desires. He exhibited reasonable behavior.

Pulling Grace down on the froufrou divan Mrs. Cabilla had brought from France and pressing his mouth to the thin, tanned line of her collarbone was not reasonable behavior. So why did he want to do it so damned much?

"Doc!"

"What?" Dan blinked, and the image of him and her on the divan went away. Poof, just like the dream bubble in a cartoon.

Before Grace could say anything more, the lights in the mansion clicked off.

"Hey!" Grace said, as if Dan had somehow turned them off to spite her.

The sound of a car's engine made Dan turn back to the window just in time to see taillights disappear down the long lane toward the poor excuse for a highway that led to town. He pressed his nose to the glass and turned his head. Both his car and Grace's were still parked in front of the house, which meant Perry had taken off and left them alone. *Weird.*

Grace joined him at the window; her shoulder brushed his bicep. Very few women's shoulders came to his elbow, and Dan found he liked having Grace's head so close to his own. If he leaned down just so, turned his head this way—

"What happened?"

Poof, there went that image, too. Dan sighed. He was getting pathetic. "Perry must have gotten tired of waiting."

"So he shut the electricity off before he left?"

Dan shrugged, and his arm slid along hers. The sexual shiver created by the contact of bare skin against bare skin, revealed by short-sleeved summer garments, made him hold his breath. Grace must have felt something too because she stepped away too quickly, too deliberately, breaking the connection of flesh on flesh.

"Uh, I guess we'd better go then."

He followed her through the darkened house toward the front door. They stepped onto the porch, the summer breeze pleasant after the heat of the day. The season had been dry, bad for farmers, great for tourists. No water meant no mosquitoes, and the mosquitoes could get so thick in the summer you couldn't get from your car to your house without being attacked by a plague worse than locusts.

Grace headed for her car, and Dan stood on the porch for a long moment and watched her move. Out here in the middle of nowhere with Grace, Dan was having strange thoughts—thoughts he'd never entertained in his staid, productive little world.

Her dress shone silver in the light of the half moon. The stark red of the sash against the brilliance of the white should have looked harsh against the subdued hues of the lake, and the trees, and the sky, but instead they looked just right. For Grace.

Dan followed, unable to help himself. That skirt, with the slit all the way up the side, enticed him as nothing else ever had. He wondered how much of her leg would be revealed when she got into her car.

But instead of going to the car, Grace meandered nearer to the lake, staring at a ripple across the surface of the water. The breeze picked up a strand of her hair and unfurled it in his direction. The scent of Grace washed over him and his body responded, as usual.

"We seem to be in a bit of a jam," she said.

She didn't know the half of it. Just in case she turned to see what was keeping him, and saw something else, Dan moved behind her.

She tilted her head and looked at the sky. "Did you ever wish on a star?"

The woman changed subjects at the speed of light. "No."

"Never?"

Star wishing had not been encouraged in his family. Wishing was for losers. Doers got the prize. "What would be the point?"

"When you wish, your dreams come true."

"Yeah, right."

"Don't you believe in anything, Dan?"

"I believe in science."

"That's all?"

He thought a moment. "Pretty much."

"Well, I'll do whatever I have to, to make my dream come true."

"Even wish on a hundred stars?"

"Whatever it takes."

In that they were alike. He'd do whatever it took to make his dream come true. But Dan knew when you wished, you only wasted time. From the way Grace was gazing up at the star-studded night, explaining his view to her would only waste more time. So he let the wishing argument go.

Grace lowered her head and gave a sigh that wavered in the middle. Before he could think about what he was doing Dan put his hands on her shoulders. Instead of stiffening, or pulling away, she went very still.

"That's my lab across the lake." His voice sounded normal. Amazing, when his body was anything but.

"The old scout camp." Her voice sounded strangled, as if she couldn't quite force the words past whatever blocked her throat. Dan's thumbs rubbed along the bend in her neck and she caught her breath.

He shouldn't touch her. Touching her was an incredible mistake. Feeling the shift of her bones beneath the dress, beneath her skin, was a bigger mistake. Being aroused even more by the heat of her in his hands, the scent of her in his nose, the need for her taste in his mouth, was insanity.

But with the moon half full, and himself completely aroused, Dan ignored his voice of reason and listened to the voice of lunacy instead.

When she turned in his arms and tilted her chin to look into his eyes, that perfect brow scrunched up and her mouth irresistibly puckered, he closed the small gap of space between them and took what he'd been wanting to take since he'd seen her only hours before.

She tasted like lemon drops and sunshine. Silly thoughts, but his mind was full of them. Of how she suddenly smelled like summer rain and winter pine. How her hands were soft on his face, then hard at the back of his neck, pulling him closer, deeper into her.

Her mouth opened, or maybe his did, but they joined with a groan that floated away on the silent night. Lips and tongues meeting, melding, magically, as if they'd been searching for each other for a very long time.

Four

Grace had always enjoyed being kissed by a man who knew what he was doing, but they were so few and far between. Amazingly, Dr. Dan was quite skilled. She'd never have known it by talking to him. Stiffs usually went—well, quite stiff, when sex was involved. Grace shifted in his arms. Her hip bumped his groin.

Hmm, stiff in more ways than one.

Dan started and would have pulled away, but Grace was not done yet. She pressed herself farther into his arms, mouth to mouth, chest to ribs, hips to thighs. Rarely did she meet a man who fit her as well as this one did. And as an extra, added plus, when his mouth was occupied upon hers he wasn't talking. When Dan talked he annoyed her, but when he kissed. . . .

"Mmm," she murmured against his lips, then ran her tongue along his teeth. Her palm cupped the back of his head, holding his mouth to hers, unwilling to let him go—yet.

Being a massage therapist attuned Grace to the sensual order of life. In order to heal, you had to feel with your hands the mysteries of the body. If you were any good, you became sensitive in the extreme. To touch, to taste, to smell.

She ran her tongue, hard, down the center of his. He shuddered and gathered her closer, tighter. She tasted mint; she smelled lake water and faded sunshine; she opened her fingers and ran them through his hair.

He had the most incredibly soft hair she'd ever touched and it was much longer than the average doctor's. Heck, much longer than the average man's, especially if you counted Olaf of the biweekly buzz cut. The only men who wore their hair longer were related to her, and since Grace just couldn't see the good doctor wearing a ponytail, or a braid, she figured this was as long as his hair got. Too bad, because she really liked that hair.

How long had it been since she'd been kissed? Far too long because she didn't want to stop. She was losing herself in him. She wanted more, and more would be a very bad idea. Sleeping with Dr. Chadwick would screw up more than her head.

Grace pulled back from the intense embrace, kissing him gently one last time because she couldn't help herself. Those lips made magic. Grace had always sensed things about people; still, she never would have figured Dan for a kissing wonder.

Em always told her nerds did it better because they tried harder. Em's third husband—or had it been the fourth?—had been an inventor with an IQ that made Grace's look puny. When he wasn't blowing up the basement, he'd been fashioning Em into a sexual savant. Her aunt hadn't been the same since.

Grace's eyes opened slowly, as if the lids were stuck together, and she stared at Dan in the pale moonlight. His eyes stayed closed, his lips looked ravished—wet, and swollen, and red. Had she done that?

Her fingers still tangled in his hair; his palms still rested along the curve of her spine. The thin, cotton dress did little to stop the heat of his hands from molding her skin against his. They might as well have been naked, since she could feel everything, and no doubt, so could he.

Their bodies pressed together, his arousal hit her just above the pelvis. She resisted the nearly irresistible urge to press against him and ignite the embrace to another level. Just because she hadn't had sex in—oh, say, half a decade—didn't mean she was going to encourage a near-stranger to make it with her on the shore of Lake Illusion—even if he wasn't a complete stranger. She had, after all, seen him naked.

The image burst to life in her brain, arousing her further. He had an incredible body, and she wanted him to hold it against hers. That was always her problem. She wanted what she could not, should not, have. That wanting had gotten her into trouble more often than not. For an instant, she remembered another lake, another man, another heartbreak.

She must have stiffened in his arms, because Dan's eyes popped open, and he stared at her as if trying to see into her brain. Grace stared back. Hey, *he'd* kissed *her.* Even if she'd kissed him back, a lot, he'd just better not—

". . . apologize."

—do that. She hated when they did that. Right now Dan looked shocked, as if he'd been caught boffing the maid.

Grace's lips pressed together, and she tasted Dan upon them. Her eyes narrowed, and she stepped back, breaking his hold upon her. Her hands unclasped, tangled again in the hair that reached to his nape, and the softness of the strands enticed her to wrap her fingers in them once more. She wanted to hold him close and kiss him more deeply, nearly as much as she wanted to slug him. She resisted both behaviors—barely.

He watched her, eyes wary; he wasn't so dumb, or perhaps merely more attuned to feelings than she'd thought. Grace turned and stalked toward her car. Dan followed on her heels.

"Grace, wait." She kept on going. "I'm sorry." She growled. "I-I mean, I'm not."

She spun around with her fists upon her hips. He stopped before he rammed into her back and knocked her into the next county. "Which is it? Sorry or not?"

He tilted his head and stared at her for a long, contemplative moment. "Which would you like?"

Her lips twitched. Definitely not so dumb, after all. Still, she wasn't going to let him off so easily. Dan was after her dream, and if she started to like him too much, she might just let him take it without a fight.

That could not happen. Too many little people needed Project Hope—and little, sick people were what mattered to Grace. Not the curve of Dan's lips, the scent of his skin, the tangle of his golden hair beneath the silver moonlight.

She cursed and yanked open the door of her car, leaping inside to get away from him. He caught the door and held on with his typical, superior strength, tugging outward while she pulled inward."Let go," she demanded.

"No. Not until you tell me why you're so mad. Is it the grant?"

"Partly."

"What's the other part?"

They both held on to the car door, as if afraid to let go and allow the other one to win even the smallest tug-of-war. Grace sighed. It was going to be a very long three weeks.

She wasn't about to tell Dan that his blasted apology had reminded her of the last man she'd taken to her bed. The last man who had broken her heart. The last man she'd vowed ever would. A man who had always apologized for touching her as if wanting her were his deepest, darkest, guiltiest secret—which had turned out to be the truth.

"Grace?" Dan's hand slid along the door, and he rested his big, warm fingers atop her smaller, cold hand.

She started at the contrast and would have yanked her hand free, then he rubbed his thumb along the hollow of hers and the gesture soothed her speeding pulse. How could the man set her heart a-racing with one touch, then calm it with the next?

"I didn't mean—"

"What? To kiss me?"

He frowned. "No. I didn't mean to upset you. I *meant* to kiss you."

"Why? You can't think I'd give in for a kiss."

"Give in?"

"Give up the grant."

"That's not why I kissed you." He frowned. "Is that why you kissed me?"

His voice had that lost quality again, which kept her from snapping "yes," a lie to soothe herself.

Could Dan really be this gentle? This sweet? This utterly clueless?

Probably, which meant Grace was in big trouble. Lost boys were her specialty. She couldn't resist a sad-eyed male.

Before he could entice her any further away from her goals, Grace yanked the door from his grasp. It slammed with a bang, and she clicked the lock shut. Then she pushed her key into the ignition and twisted her wrist, planning to spin out of Mrs. Cabilla's drive and leave Dan in the dark.

The only problem with her plan was that when she turned the key in the ignition, nothing happened. Grace rested her forehead on the steering wheel.

Tap, tap, tap.

She turned her head to the side. Dan's face hovered in the dark outside the window. "Need a ride?"

Dan wasn't sure what he'd done to make her so mad. He'd tried to be a gentleman, after nearly turning into an animal, and she'd acted like he'd done just the opposite.

She'd kissed him back, damn it! She'd kissed him back and liked it. She had not flinched from his body's response to her. She'd welcomed him, wooed him, wanted him. Or at least when her mouth had been against his, he'd believed that. Now he wasn't so sure. With Grace, Dan wasn't sure about anything.

She was earth and fire, woman and passion—different from anyone Dan had ever known. He wanted to know more, even though she'd probably kick his teeth down his throat if he tried.

As he watched her get out of the car, and discovered how the slit in her white skirt skimmed back from her bronzed thigh, Dan thought a kick in the teeth might just be worth one more kiss.

He followed Grace across the driveway toward his pickup truck. Before he could open the door for her, she did it herself and got inside. Unfortunately the position of the door kept Dan from watching her skirt again. He really liked that skirt.

Can't have everything, although something, once in awhile, would be nice, Dan thought.

Abstinence had been his choice for a long time. He had priorities, and women were far down the list. He hadn't minded—until today. Why, suddenly, with this woman, did he think of nothing but tumbled sheets, naked bodies, and the scent of her all over him?

With a sigh of disappointment, tinged with exasperation, Dan crossed to the driver's side and got in. Grace perched as close as she could get to the passenger door, as if she'd leap out if he so much as slid an inch closer. Dan was used to people keeping their distance from him, because of both his size and social ineptitude, so why did Grace's distance hurt?

Maybe because he wanted nothing more than for her to slide across the bench seat and cuddle up against his shoulder as he drove her home—like the conclusion of a date to a drive-in movie?

Dan shook his head at his own foolishness. He'd never been to a drive-in movie. Heck, he hadn't been on that many dates. As a kid, he'd been too big and awkward for the girls to like. While he was still big, though less awkward, dating didn't appear like very grown-up behavior, even if he had the guts to go trolling for women in Lake Illusion.

"This doesn't seem like your kind of car," Grace ventured.

Dan glanced her way. She still hugged the door, but if she wanted to try polite conversation, he was game. "No? What does? A Ferrari?" He'd always wanted one—fancy, exotic, sleek—three things Dan Chadwick could never be.

"No." That single word deflated his fantasy. He should have known Grace didn't see him as a Ferrari kind of guy. Her gaze wandered over his large body, and she bit her lip, concentrating. His eyes fixed upon white teeth against russet lips and stuck there. Her mouth moved. "Not a Porsche, either."

Pop went the fantasy of nibbling that lip himself. Dan snorted. In a Porsche he'd resemble a sardine in a can. That's why he had a pickup—a big guy's car—meant to get him where he needed to be, any time he needed to be there. Even in the dead of a north woods winter when hardly anyone got anywhere, ever.

"Maybe a Lincoln," she said. "Navy blue."

Dan scowled. His father had a navy blue Cadillac—too close for comfort. "Not up here," he said.

"Then one of those fancy four-by-fours—a Navigator, an Expedition."

"A car's a car," he said, a bit irritably, as he reached under the floor mat for his key.

"Not really. My father and I always played this game when I was a child." Her voice took on a dreamy quality as she remembered. "We lived in a town very like Lake Illusion. On sunny summer days we would sit downtown, pick a tourist, then try and figure out what kind of car they drove. Dad was very good at the game."

"Was?"

"He died about eight years ago."

"Sorry."

She shrugged. "Long time passing."

"So how come he was so good at the car game?"

"Figuring out why people did what they did, what they were hiding, if they were lying, that was his job."

A sudden insight dawned. "He was a lawyer."

Grace rewarded him with a smile. Dan resisted the urge to stick out his chest and preen.

"Yes, from the inside out. When we played the car game it was one of the few times he played with me, and I ate up the attention. It wasn't until years later that I realized observing people wasn't a game to him but practice. And he was right. A car says quite a bit about the owner if you take the time to look."

Dan glanced through the windshield at her leaf-green Bronco. "If that's true, then your car doesn't match you either."

Her lips curved a bit, and she sat up straighter, away from the door and closer to him. Perhaps small talk wasn't such a bad idea if it made Grace relax. And he liked hearing about her family. Not only was Grace different from any woman he'd ever known, but her family was fascinating, too. He'd never been interested in people before. Maybe he just hadn't met the right people.

"Why doesn't my car match me?"

"If anyone should own a Ferrari it should be you."

She tilted her head. "Why?"

Didn't she look in a mirror? "You're so, so . . ."

"What?"

The word was clipped, irritated. Dan wasn't sure what he'd done now. "Beautiful, exotic, sleek, and lovely."

He was proud he'd gotten those words out without stumbling over a few, and proud he'd complimented her without being asked. In his former world, women adored compliments. He'd never quite mastered the knack of giving them, though.

Grace's face went still, all the animation of their silly conversation wiped free, and she glanced out the window away from him. Somehow he'd screwed up again. "How I look has nothing to do with who I am," she murmured.

Hmm, Dan thought, *a woman after my own heart.*

How many times had he felt just the same when judged upon his appearance?

He wanted to apologize, but apologizing seemed to be a bad idea with Grace. He wanted to reach across the distance and touch her, but in the close confines of the cab, touching her would be a bad idea, too. If he touched her, even a bit, he'd want to do a whole lot more.

Instead, he said softly, "You have a Ferrari inside, too, Grace. Top of the line."

She turned and studied him for a long moment, as if she were seeing him for the very first time. "How would you know?"

How *did* he know? Like he was such a great judge of character when he spent most of his time with bottles and beakers? Today was the first day he'd ventured into Lake Illusion in months, and one of the reasons he did what he did was that he wasn't very good with people. Call it a curse—his parents certainly did.

Studying Grace's intent face, Dan wondered why his second compliment seemed to matter more to her than the first. In his experience, having a Ferrari inside was not as important as having a Ferrari outside. Where he came from, having a Ferrari at all was the important thing.

"Dan?" She wasn't going to give up. "How would you know anything about my inside, except in a medical chart sort of way?"

He shrugged, hesitated, then told a truth that surprised him. "I just know. Call it a feeling."

A small smile lit her face. All was forgiven, just like that. He blinked at the sudden change. Every woman he'd ever known held on to a grudge and worked the thing for all it was worth. And they would never have let him off the hook with that "feeling" defense, even if it was the truth.

"I couldn't afford a toy Ferrari," she said, "let alone a real one."

Dan put the key into the ignition. "In that we're the same."

"Really?" Her brow creased. "I pegged you for a wealthy guy."

Dan's heart did a slow roll, and his hand fell back to his knee. "Why would you think that?"

"You have the air of the raised rich."

She was right, but he hated that she'd seen it. The environment in which he'd been raised was nothing to brag about. That was another reason he was a researcher, and also why his parents had disinherited him years ago. He was an embarrassment to them. He did, however, miss his little sister.

"You've seen a lot of the raised rich, have you?"

"Yes, I have. Look around you, Doctor. Lake Illusion is a tourist town—the playground of the wealthy who look for a place to pretend they're in the woods."

Dan peered into the dark of the trees surrounding them. "Looks like the woods to me."

"Out here it is, but that's only because Mrs. Cabilla has enough money to keep it that way. Back there . . ." She pointed at the distant lights of the city. "Nature is just an illusion."

Dan didn't know what to say to that, so he just nodded, then turned the key. Nothing happened.

They both turned to look at each other with their mouths hanging open.

"Uh-oh," Dan said.

"Yeah, uh-oh. A bit too much of a coincidence, wouldn't you say?"

"Yes." Dan stared at the dark house, remembering how the electricity had gone off right before Perry's car disappeared down the drive. What was the little weasel up to?

"Aren't you going to check on the car?"

"Me?" He glanced at her wide-eyed.

"Maybe you can fix it."

"Me?"

"You're a guy, aren't you?"

"Last I looked."

"Last I looked, too."

Dan's face heated, and he thanked all that was holy that night had fallen so she could not see. He blushed like a schoolgirl, which was embarrassing when you were built like a linebacker.

Dan opened the car and got out. "Guess I could look under the hood." For all the good it would do. He'd never looked under a hood in his life.

"Don't you have to pop it open?"

"Okay." Dan shrugged and reached back in to pull the hood release. The front popped up with a dull thump.

Once he had the hood open and secure, Dan stared into the engine. There was just enough light from the half moon to make the metal shine silver. Grace joined him, and they stared at it together.

"So what do you think?" she asked.

"That's an engine all right."

"You really have no idea, do you?"

"Not a one."

"I thought you were some brilliant scientist."

"Scientist, not mechanic."

She grunted, unimpressed. "If you're such a genius, you'd think you could fix a car."

"You'd think."

Dan refused to allow the feeling of inadequacy stealing over him to take root. Just because he was a klutz at life didn't mean he had to hang his head. He was a genius—at medical science. Fat lot of good that did him right now.

"Got a cell phone?" She took a step toward the truck as if she expected him to answer in the affirmative.

"No."

Grace stopped and turned toward him. "You don't? What kind of doctor are you?"

"One who doesn't have patients."

"Good point. Don't you ever have to call anyone?"

"Never had to make a call that couldn't wait until I reached a phone. Until right this minute anyway. Don't you have one?"

"There aren't too many massage emergencies. Besides I'm against them on principle. My job is stress reduction. Phones going off at all hours, people running around with phones pressed to their ears at the supermarket, Little League, in the car. . . ." She shuddered. "It's like something out of a horror movie. Attack of the killer cell phones."

He smiled at the image. He'd always thought the same thing.

After a moment of staring at each other, they sighed, and turned toward the house together. The dark windows stared back at them like mocking eyes. "No electric, no phone," Dan observed.

"We could wait inside."

"Until morning?"

"I guess. Perry will come back, won't he?"

"If he left us here for nefarious reasons . . ." What those reasons could be Dan had no idea, but when he got his hands on weasel boy he would find out. "He isn't coming back."

Grace crossed the driveway and turned the front doorknob. Locked.

Dan joined her on the porch. "If we broke a window, would an alarm go off?"

"What alarm?"

"There isn't an alarm?"

"What for?"

"Protection? A theft deterrent?"

"Out here? Most people don't even lock their doors."

"I do."

"You would. But you're one of the few."

"There are strangers all over the place."

"Tourists. You think they spend their summer vacation robbing little old ladies?"

"Still . . ."

Grace shrugged. "I suggested an alarm to Mrs. Cabilla once and she refused. She said she didn't want nature spoiled with bells and whistles."

"That's crazy."

"She's in the Andes Mountains looking for sheep. Does that seem logical to you?"

The girl had a point. "So what do we do now?" he asked.

"Now"—Grace gazed up at the stars—"we walk to your place."

Five

"My place?" Dan's voice rose in surprise, and he squinted across the water at the pinprick of light amidst a great, big dark. "But my place is on the other side of the lake. Is there a boat?"

"Even if there is, rowing across is harder than walking around. And I don't know anything about motorboats. Do you?"

"Sailboats," he mumbled, as if sailing were a crime.

"That we definitely don't have." Grace stepped off the porch and started toward the twin dead cars.

"Wait a minute." When she didn't stop, he followed her. "You said we'd walk. How are we going to walk?"

"You've got feet."

"This lake is ten miles around."

Grace resisted the urge to roll her eyes. She'd been doing that so much lately she was going to roll them right out of her head.

Dan might live here, he might work here; he might even like it here; but Dan was a city boy from the tip of his bare, blond head to the toe of his brand-name sneakers. At least he could walk a mile—make that several—in those shoes, and the sun had gone down, so he wouldn't get heat exhaustion or sunburn from walking around without a hat.

"Why don't we go out to the road?" Warily he eyed the mountain-sized pine trees. "Maybe we can flag a ride."

"The road is the long way. And no one's out there at this time of night."

"Why not? It's a road, isn't it?"

"Yeah, County Highway to nowhere. Listen, there's nothing out this way but the lake, which is private, and a lot more trees than you would ever believe. All the tourist action is on the other side of town. The locals go to bed early so they can get up and fish, work, or serve the masses."

Dan continued to contemplate the dark forest. "So you plan to go through there?"

"It's the only way."

Grace pulled her sneakers out of the car and tossed the sandals back inside. She grabbed the spare flashlight and tucked it into her belt. Standing on one foot, she braced her hand against the car and slipped into the well-worn shoes. When she turned around she bumped into Dan, which was like walking into a tall, cushy wall.

Her butt slammed against the door handle, and she hissed in both pain and annoyance at the thought of the lovely bruise she would have in a place the sun didn't shine—or at least didn't shine anymore. Sunbathing nude had lost its appeal the first time one of the low-flying gliders from the municipal airport had skimmed past her roof. She might be free-spirited, but an exhibitionist she was not.

"Sorry," Dan said. "I didn't mean to startle you. What are you doing?"

"Getting ready to walk a few miles."

"You keep sneakers in the car?" He acted like she kept loco weed under the seat.

"Doesn't everyone?" Grace started across the driveway at a brisk pace. Dan could keep up or be left behind.

"Not where I come from," he muttered.

Grace had no doubt about that. Where he came from tennis shoes were used for tennis, and you didn't keep them in the backseat of the limo.

The man came from money. Big money, most likely. Which only made his insistence that he needed the Cabilla Grant to cure para . . . pora . . . whatever it was, a line of hooey and made Grace feel a whole lot less guilty for planning to take the money from him. He could just use his trust fund, or trot home to Mummy and use hers.

Crunch, crunch went the loose stones at the side of the driveway.

Mumble, grumble went Dan's voice beneath his breath. *Shuffle, scuffle, shuffle and scuffle* went his feet as he hurried to catch up with her.

Grace pulled out the flashlight and flicked her thumb over the button. A garish yellow beam invaded the soft silver path of moonlight, but she had little choice. Once beneath the dense cover of the forest, they would be unable to see. They didn't want to run into a tree—or worse.

Entering the woods, Dan stepped right on a fallen

branch. The resounding crack made an owl start up from a nearby tree. Small, furry things fled. Something heavy, but fleet, took off in another direction, smashing bushes and branches in its haste to get away from the klutz who had invaded their night.

Grace's *nimishoomis,* her grandfather, had always said white men walked heavier than wounded buffaloes and made more noise than grizzlies on a rampage. Not that there were any grizzlies in Wisconsin, but the point was the same. At this rate, Grace wouldn't have to worry about any animal of the woods catching them unaware. They'd all be on the other side of the lake, running away from Dan, the destructor.

"Is there a trail from one side of this lake to the other?" Dan interrupted her thoughts.

"No."

Dan stopped. Grace kept going. He hurried to catch up again and slid on the wet grass where it grew thick, sleek, and long beneath the cover of the towering trees.

His arms flew up and he smacked one into a bush. Twigs flew every which way, showering Grace's hair and raining down onto the ground. Dan stepped on those, too—*snap, crackle, pop.*

"Grace!" he shouted.

A raccoon chattered. Grace flashed the beam of light at the sound and pinned the animal in a golden circle where he scolded them from the crook of a tree. Dan leapt in front of Grace. He was really very sweet.

She put her free hand on his arm. "I don't think he's dangerous, just a little mad at you."

The muscles beneath her fingers tensed, hardened. Grace resisted the urge to push on them, stroke and separate, soothe and smooth. Muscles, skin, and bone were her specialty and she rarely got to touch a specimen such as Dan.

He straightened and the damp rubber sole of his shoe made a squeaking, squishing sound against the grass. The raccoon growled and scrambled higher in the tree. "What's *he* mad about?"

"You scared him."

He looked sideways and the beam hit his eyes, making him squint and wince, just like the raccoon. Grace lowered the light to the ground. "How could I scare him when I didn't even know he was there?"

The guy was clueless but still sweet. Imagine, jumping in front of her like a knight to protect her from Rocky Raccoon.

"You're awfully loud, Dan."

"Me?"

Definitely clueless.

He stepped back and swept out his hand in a gallant, though sarcastic, gesture. "Lead on. I'll try to be more quiet."

That would be like a Mack truck trying to sneak down a country gravel road, but Grace kept her opinion to herself and led on. Dan scrambled to stay at her side. The woods had gone silent. Every living thing must have scattered already.

"Raccoons, and squirrels, and bears—"

"Oh, my," Grace muttered.

Dan laughed. Point for him. "*Are* there bears in these woods?"

"Sure."

"Ever seen one?"

"Uh-huh." Grace remembered the first time. The bear had scrambled up a tree almost as fast as she had run the other way.

"Think we'll see one tonight?" Another branch broke beneath his feet.

"No way."

"Hmm." He sounded both disappointed and relieved. Grace had to smile. City folk were fascinated by bears. Guess you didn't see too many from high-rise windows. "You're sure you know where you're going?" Dan said.

"I'm sure."

"You walk these woods a lot?"

"Not these."

But some just like them. As a child she'd spent time with her paternal grandparents, at her mother's insistence. Even as her father gave his life for the rights of his people, he would have let his daughter grow up ignorant of all that was Ojibway. He wanted her to be who she was. He had never understood that part of who she was was just that.

Ignorance of the customs did not make her skin any lighter. Being half Irish did not make people stare at her any less. Knowing who she came from, and why that was important, was all that had made the tough times bearable. Her mother had understood that and sent her to her grandparents for part of every summer.

With them she learned to love the forest, and that love had never died. Tall buildings made her claustrophobic, flat places made her feel exposed, deserts were, well, deserted. Whenever she was away she ached for green rolling hills, sun on water, and snow heavy upon the pines. Bad memories had made her flee, but good memories brought her back.

Dan stopped. "Where are you from?"

Grace kept going. A breeze blew the hair back from her face, and she breathed deeply of the air, scenting rain, and a spark of electricity. No time to dawdle. She didn't want to be in the woods when the coming storm broke.

"A place south and east of here."

A place she had not been able to return to because all her bad memories lingered there.

Dan double-timed to catch up with her again. "You lived on the reservation?"

"No." For some reason outsiders always figured every Indian in town had escaped from the reservation. She waited for him to ask *why not?* but for once he kept quiet.

The woods thickened and the going slowed. Their feet slid along the damp forest cover. Here, the ground remained wet well into August. The sun rarely reached past the blanket of trees to dry the ground from the winter snows and the spring rains. Purple flowers grew amidst the grass. The woodsy, wild scent of mushrooms and moss warred with the aroma of pine needles and sap.

Neither the moon nor the stars could be seen any longer. Grace reached into her pocket and pulled out a compass, flicking the beam across its face. She gave a sharp nod. She'd thought they were still headed in the right direction, but in the woods it paid to be certain.

"You've got a compass?" Dan sounded so amazed that Grace smiled.

"Doesn't everyone?" She popped the circlet back into her pocket.

"I didn't think *you'd* need a compass."

Grace's smile faded. "And why wouldn't I?'

"Don't you just know inherently where you are, where to go?"

Annoyance flashed through her. "Knowing how to get from here to there doesn't come from my blood but from my brain. If you live in these woods, you need to know how to survive in these woods. Cars fail all the time. And a casual stroll can turn deadly if you don't know what you're doing."

"I've offended you again."

Grace sighed. She shouldn't get so defensive, but some things never changed, and of all people, she'd thought Dan would not judge her by her cover since he didn't like being judged by his.

"Never mind," she said. "We need to hurry if we don't want to be caught in the storm."

"Storm?" Dan lengthened his strides to keep up with her trot. "What storm? The weather report said clear, no clouds."

She couldn't help it. She just *had* to roll her eyes. "You listen to the weather report?"

"Doesn't everyone?" He threw her own words back at her. She didn't take the bait.

"Sure, but they don't actually believe it."

"Then how do you know there's a storm coming?"

"Inherent weather-predicting ability," she said and plunged into the darkest part of the forest.

* * *

Dan walked faster, keeping one eye on the hide-and-seek white of Grace's dress through the trees and the other on the shadows, searching for bears. Grace didn't seem to think there were any about, but Dan wasn't so sure. She also thought it was going to storm, and there hadn't been a cloud in the sky when they entered the woods.

A tree branch slapped Dan in the face, yanking him from his reverie. He really was out of his element here, while Grace seemed completely at home. This *was* her home. He wished it had always been his.

Dan had been born and raised in Phoenix, Arizona. He'd never fit in there. For some reason neither the arid, dry desert nor the mountains surrounding the city appealed to him. Here, the whisper of the wind through the trees calmed him and the lakes soothed. The coolness in the air, every morning and every evening, made Dan feel more alive than he'd ever felt before. He should have been born here—like Grace.

Dan blinked. He'd lost sight of her white dress while lost in thought. He hurried to catch up. The forest closed in around him, the foliage at his back thicker, the trees up ahead taller, the brush on the sides denser. Dan had no idea where he was or which way Grace had gone.

Drawing a deep breath, he opened his mouth to shout her name, then hesitated. Grace said he was too loud. Perhaps because bears responded to screaming tourists just as sharks were drawn to the vibrations and gyrations of swimmers? He snapped his mouth closed.

He would just keep going straight ahead. How hard could walking in a straight line be?

Pretty hard, Dan discovered. Nothing looked straight in the dark. If he came across a fallen tree he had to climb under, go over, or inch around it. Grace had taken the flashlight with her. Where the beam had seemed bright and shiny at his side, now he could see no hint of the light around anywhere. He became disoriented. After what seemed like hours, but was probably only ten minutes, Dan panicked and stopped in a tiny clearing.

Why, oh, why had he allowed himself to lose sight of Grace? Why had she left him behind to die?

Dan laughed to himself. "So melodramatic."

"Who?" asked an owl.

Dan jumped at the sound. Why couldn't he get used to the noises of the flora and fauna of the forest?

The sound of something crashing through the brush in his direction made Dan wish he'd kept his mouth shut—and stayed in Arizona. He might not be used to the noises out here, but he knew what a large, lumbering body sounded like.

Maybe he wasn't being so melodramatic after all. Maybe he *was* going to die here. Maybe Grace had planned this whole thing. In fact, that made more sense than Perry, the weasel, leaving them in a lurch. And who had been prepared for this little jaunt, with shoes in her car, flashlight in the glove compartment, and a compass in her pocket? Grace, that's who.

And why? With Dan out of the way, Grace got the grant.

Another crunch and a crash, closer, made Dan push aside conspiracy theories for the moment. He had more pressing concerns. Such as—should he climb a tree?

As if he could. The trees in this part of the forest were huge, with little in the way of footholds, and far too big for even a guy of his size to put his arms around and shimmy up. Even if he could climb one, Dan remembered hearing on the Discovery Channel that bears could climb better and quicker than people. They could also run pretty fast—especially if they were chasing something. What you were supposed to do if a bear showed up was pretend you were dead.

No problem there. Dan was just about ready for a heart attack.

He dropped to the ground, curled himself into a ball, with his knees beneath his chest and his hands clasped behind his head. He made a pretty large target, but if he was lucky maybe the bear was on its way to a honey tree and would run right by.

No such luck for Dan, but then he'd never been very lucky. Thunder rumbled in the distance, like an omen. The animal crashed into the small clearing, ran across the grass—and tripped over Dan, landing right next to his head.

Dan tensed, waiting for teeth and claws to tear him apart. Instead he caught the scent of Grace and raised his head. Their noses brushed, she was that close. Relief flashed through him a moment before the anger in her eyes made him wonder if his pan-

icked ramblings were true. She looked mad enough
to kill. But she really wasn't the type, was she?

"I'm going to kill you, Dr. Chadwick."

Hmm, maybe she was. Look at Ted Bundy, Jeffrey
Dahlmer and John Wayne Gacy. Mild-mannered-
looking guys one and all. Not every murderer had
"crazy" tattooed on their forehead like Manson. Too
bad.

Slowly Dan sat up, slid away from her. At least
there was no bear—at the moment—though perhaps he'd be better off if there were.

"You wanna calm down, Grace?"

"Don't tell me to calm down!" Her voice had a
shrill edge.

"All right." He held up his hands in a gesture of
surrender. "I won't."

She stood and her skirt swirled about her ankles.
Since he was still on the ground, he got an extensive
flash of skin, too. He couldn't help it, his gaze went
to her leg and stuck there.

Snap, snap. She clicked her fingers in front of his
face. "Doc? Stay with me." She held out her hand.
He just stared at that, too.

"Get up, you're all wet."

Actually he wasn't, but he probably would be
soon. Thunder rumbled again. The storm he hadn't
believed was coming, came.

He climbed to his feet without her help, as if she
could pull him to his feet. When he stood, she put
her hands on her hips and scowled. "You scared me
half to death," she accused.

"Me? You left me alone to die in the woods with
the bears."

"There aren't any bears."

"But you said—"

She cut him off with an exasperated sound. "All right, there are, but now that you've knocked down half the forest, they aren't anywhere near here. Bears are more afraid of us than we are of them."

"Then why—?"

"I was playing with your head."

Dan rarely got mad. He just wasn't a guy with much of a temper. So few things were worth getting angry over. Because of his size he'd always worried about what he might do if he got too angry. Right now, with the tang of terror fresh upon his tongue, he just didn't care.

"You let me believe there might be bears lurking behind every tree, then left me out here? I might have had a heart attack. Or was that what you were hoping for?"

She scowled. "I didn't *leave* you anywhere. You couldn't keep up. Besides, I was sitting on your porch. All you had to do was walk straight for twenty feet. You couldn't even do that. Did you know you walked in a complete circle?"

"I did not. I stayed on a straight line. You just left me in the middle of the forest."

She stomped across the short distance separating them, grabbed his hand in surprisingly strong fingers, and yanked him after her. Ten feet, straight ahead, the forest thinned. Another ten feet and they stepped into a clearing. There sat his cabin, the lake, the camp.

Idiot.

"So if I was walking in circles, but only twenty feet

from the cabin, and there aren't any bears, why are you trembling?" he asked.

"Just because there aren't any bears doesn't mean you can't die in the woods. It happens at least once every summer and a lot every winter."

"What does?"

"A clueless tourist walks into the woods and never comes back out."

"I don't see how that could happen."

"Look." She pointed behind him.

Dan turned. The forest rose, thick and tall. Dark. Mysterious. Deadly. Where they'd walked through he could not see. It was as if a path had opened for Grace and himself, then closed. Which was impossible. Logically he knew that, but from where Dan stood he could not see any way to walk through the trees back in the direction they had come. He shivered at the implications.

Grace came up behind him, a calming presence at his back. At least he wasn't alone. "You get disoriented when everything around you is ten times taller. If you don't have a compass, and most of *you* don't"—she said *you* like she might say *naïve fools*—"you're in big trouble."

"What about the stars, the moon, the sun?"

"If they're out, and you're in a part of the forest where you can see them, would you know how to guide from them?"

Dan shrugged. "Maybe."

"Exactly. And you're Dan, the Wonder Doctor— think about some regular Joe out here. They'd be toast within a few days."

"Don't you have trackers, dogs, cops?"

"Sure. We've even got Indian guides. But if they don't know you're missing, or where you went in, it makes things kind of tough."

Dan stared at the woods, while Grace took his hand once more. He didn't want her to let go, so he held her fingers loosely, and didn't move a single iota. "What should I do then, if I get lost again?"

"Hug a tree."

"What?" He glanced at her but she wasn't laughing. At least not so he could tell. "I thought you said hug a tree."

"That's right. Haven't you ever seen Barney? He gives good advice."

"Barney? Is he some north woods survivalist?"

"He's a giant purple dinosaur."

Had she been smoking funny-smelling weed while he wandered in circles? Dan moved closer and peered into her face to observe how big her pupils were. From what he could see in the shadows, she looked fine. She still smelled like Grace and nothing else—sexy, sinful, scrumptious. Maybe he'd taken in too much night magic himself.

Grace grinned. *"Barney* is a kid's television show."

"You watch kid's television a lot?"

Her grin faded. "At hospitals. Yes."

Dan cursed himself for wiping the smile from her face. He suspected she'd watched television with some very sick kids while they held blankets from Project Hope. A twinge of guilt came over Dan, but he refused to allow it to take root. He needed that grant. He was too close to a cure to give up now.

"And this amazing dinosaur says to hug a tree if you're lost in the woods."

"Yes. Stay where you are. Don't wander. Then someone can find you more easily. If you go in circles"—she raised an eyebrow at him—"you end up deeper in the forest and it's harder to find you when you cross your own trail again and again."

Slowly, Dan nodded. "Easy enough and it makes sense. So did you learn all this from Barney? Or did you learn some from your dad?"

"My dad?" Her voice rose in amazement. "Why would my dad know anything about the forest?"

"He's Ojibway."

"So? I don't think he stepped foot in the woods after he stepped into college."

The way she said that made Dan think she didn't approve, and he had to wonder why. But before he could ask, the sky opened and poured rain on them as if it had been holding a bucket over their heads all along. Grace's white dress plastered to her body and made Dan forget all about her dad, the attorney.

He took one step toward the house, but Grace held back, turning her face up to the sky and letting the rain tumble down her cheeks. He'd have thought the droplets were tears if he hadn't heard her laugh out loud.

She let go of his hand and turned her palms up toward the raging sky, raising her arms until she stood like a sacrifice to the hidden moon. Slowly, she turned, a single, graceful revolution—a dance with the music of the night.

Dan couldn't move; he could only stare at her in wonder as his body clamored for hers.

The lack of moisture all summer had made the

ground hard everywhere but in the forest, and the sudden, unexpected abundance of water ran in rivulets along the dusty yard. Dan hadn't seen the point in watering grass that was already dead. So he possessed a yard full of dirt that would soon be mud, if the rain continued to fall.

Grace lowered her hands, lowered her head, kicked off her shoes, and wiggled her toes in the tiny river that ran by. Joy spread over her face, capturing him once again. "Ah, that feels so good after walking so long."

It was as if their argument had never happened. The terror in the woods gone, the tension between them moot. The woman lived in the moment, taking pleasure from whatever came along. Dan watched her and he wanted to do that, too. But he had no idea how.

Then she smiled at him through the rain, and his heart nearly stopped. "Take off your shoes, Doc. Live a little."

Dan stiffened. Take off his shoes? Stand in the rain? Squelch his toes through the mud?

He shrugged. Why not? Dan yanked off the two-hundred-dollar shoes his sister had given him on his last birthday, tossed them aside, and sent his socks tumbling after.

Grace was right. The rain soothed his heated feet, the dirt became mud beneath his toes, and he liked it. What he liked even more was the thought of his mother's face if she could see him right now. She'd have a kitten.

Dan laughed out loud, then threw his head back and drank of the rain and the night.

Six

For Grace the world was made up of the scent of evergreens at Christmas, the flavor of lemonade on the Fourth of July, and the softness of a baby bunny's fur at Easter. Those things were good things—tactile memories to hold in your heart and take out when life got tough.

She added another memory right then and there. The sight of Dan Chadwick in the rain—a temptation so great she didn't think she could resist. So she stood and watched the man come alive before her eyes.

The rain plastered his shirt to his chest, defining the muscles, clinging to his biceps. She wanted to touch that shirt, slip her fingers beneath the neckline, rub her knuckles along his collarbone, and press her mouth to the pulse that called her name, while peeking from between the open buttons of his shirt.

The way he'd kicked off his shoes—so stiff and jerky—as if he'd never done such a thing before, Grace had figured he wouldn't last a minute out in the rain. As soon as the first droplet hit his head he'd run for the cabin to avoid melting like the Wicked Witch of the West.

She'd waited for him to fold his socks neatly, or stuff them into his shoes. When he tossed them into the growing river of mud, he earned a three-point bonus from Grace.

The rain darkened his hair; the mud squished between his toes. She could smell Dan, an enticing combination of musk and man and one more thing she couldn't quite identify. That scent tickled the edge of her mind, just beyond the tip of her tongue, hovering, waiting. . . .

Crack!

Lightning. Electricity. *Close.* Not Dan at all, but danger. She grabbed him.

"What's the matter?" he asked.

"We're too close to the trees. Let's get inside."

"Not yet." He did a fancy two-step in the mud. "I thought we were going to live a little."

Lightning flashed. *Closer.* The trees were too great an enticement.

"There's a time to live and a time to die, which is what we'll be doing if we get barbecued because we're too dumb to come in from the rain."

She tugged on Dan's hand again, and he reluctantly took a step after her. Grace had a funny feeling at the back of her neck, as if the hair stood on end. She picked up the pace, yanking Dan along with her, not an easy task.

The acrid scent of electricity filled the air; the hair on Grace's arms tingled. Her body hummed with the energy that surrounded them. *Something wicked this way comes,* she thought, and started to run.

They'd almost reached the relative safety of the porch when Dan slid in the mud river. It was like watching someone skate on glare ice—someone who had no idea how to skate. Dan's bare feet skidded a neat double furrow in the yard, right before those feet flipped up and he fell flat on his back. Unfortunately, they were connected at the hand and Grace went down, too—right on top of Dan.

Then lightning hit where they'd been standing. The earth beneath them shook; the air sizzled. Dan dumped her unceremoniously into the mud, covering her body with his.

The ground was cool at her back. The man was warm all along her front. The wind smelled of flames and the rain. Dan had his face pressed along her neck, and when his lips moved against her skin, a prayer or maybe a curse, she shuddered.

He lifted his head and looked toward the trees. "There's a fire," he said, amazement in his voice.

Grace followed the direction of his gaze. Mud squelched into her hair. Sure enough, one of the trees at the edge of the forest had been struck and flames shot upward. But even as she watched, rain hit the fire and a hissing noise filled the air. "It's all right. The rain will put out the fire."

He turned back and lifted a mud-caked brow. "Sure?"

"Yes." Thunder rumbled in the distance. The rain slowed from a torrent to a trickle. The fire went out with a last, dying *poof*. The storm fled as quickly as it had come.

Grace became aware of a rock pressing into her rump and Dan's knee digging into her calf. What had felt good amidst the wildness of the storm had become uncomfortable as reality returned. Wasn't that always the way?

"Thank you for the gallant gesture. . . ." Grace shifted and the rock dug deeper. She shoved at Dan's shoulders. He was as immovable as that rock. "But we can get up now. The storm's gone."

The clouds drifted off, too, revealing the moon once more. A silver halo surrounded Dan's head, throwing shadows all about him and making it difficult to decipher his expression. Grace didn't see the kiss coming until his lips pressed against hers.

She forgot the rock at her back, the knee against her legs, and the weight of the man pressing her into mud that didn't feel quite so good anymore. Because, as before, the kiss certainly did.

They had mud on their faces, mud on their hands, mud all over their feet and their clothes. But it just didn't matter. All that mattered was what happened when their lips joined.

Dan's kiss was so incredibly good it had to be bad, Grace thought, even as she wrapped her arms about the broad shoulders that blocked out the moon, the stars, and the sky, and held him closer to her.

There was some reason she shouldn't be kissing this man, but she couldn't recall what that reason was. So Grace threw caution to the winds, something she was very good at, and let him kiss her while she kissed him right back.

He nibbled at her lips as if he had all night. Actually they did. Where were they going but into the cabin? And then . . .

Grace pushed away those implications so she

could enjoy the moment. There were a lot of good things about enjoying the moment, something her mother always preached, and her father never learned. That omission had killed him in the end.

Her mouth opened beneath Dan's questing tongue. He tasted of rainwater and storm wind, an arousing combination she wanted to taste again. So she swept her tongue out to meet his and they tangoed a moment or two.

He moaned as she tugged his lip into her mouth, suckling, tasting, teasing. Her fingers tangled in his hair, holding him to her because right now she did not want to let him go.

He shifted, and the weight of his body eased to the side. Now his knee pressed into her thigh—or perhaps it wasn't his knee. She shifted, too, bumping her hip along that hardness. He pulled his mouth from hers on a hiss that sounded of pain, and she murmured soothing nonsense against his jaw. His hand cupped her hip and pulled her against him— hill to valley, hard to soft, man to woman.

He resurrected their kiss; his body blotted out the night, pressing against her where she wanted him the most.

Then headlights pinned them. They had been so engrossed in what they made each other feel, as inappropriate and dangerous as it was, that they had not heard the car approach until too late.

Once again Dan put himself between Grace and danger, even though he'd be better off not to. She was the one at home here; he was merely meat if the wild animals ever got a hold of him. And the wildest animals of all did not live in the forest—as was proven by the man who climbed out of the car.

"Gracie, what are you doing rolling in the mud with this very bad man?" Olaf bellowed.

"Uh-oh," Grace murmured.

Dan glanced at her with a frown. "Uh-oh? Don't say 'Uh-oh.' "

Grace sat up. She didn't think lying on the ground was the best option at this point, although a moment ago rolling in the mud had been quite appealing. "What should I say?"

"Say I'm not a very bad man. Say this was your idea"—he stood and waved a hand at the mud puddle they'd been wrestling in—"not mine."

Now she was annoyed. He made it sound like she'd pulled him down and taken his virtue by force. Grace stood, too, and put her hands on her hips, as she spread her bare feet wide and dug her toes into the wet earth. "I'd be happy to do that, except this wasn't my idea."

"Well, it wasn't mine either. It was an accident."

"Accident? Accident?" Olaf slammed the car door. Both Grace and Dan jumped. The huge man stalked toward them. "I know what means accident. There better not have been an accident with my Gracie."

"What does he mean by 'my Gracie'? He's awfully mad for a business partner."

Grace went from annoyed to downright furious in the space of a single sentence out of Dr. Chadwick's mouth. She admitted to having a temper, but Dan seemed to have an uncommon ability to rile her. "Just what are you insinuating, Doctor?"

"I just want to know why I'm about to be torn limb from limb. Is he the irate father type, or the homicidal boyfriend?"

"Boyfriend? Are you crazy? He's over fifty."

"So? Some women like that. Just tell me and I'll step aside."

She wanted to slug him so bad her hands balled into fists. But she'd never been the violent type—until she met Dan.

What did Mama always say? Hate rides the winds of love. Perhaps anger was the other side of lust. Because while she wanted very much to slug Dr. Dan, the scent of his skin, the storm-blue of his eyes, and the memory of those clever lips also made her want to kiss him all over again.

A huge hand came down on her shoulder. "Gracie, it is time to go. No more rolling in the mud with the bad man."

"I am *not* a bad man!"

"That is a matter of opinion." Olaf sniffed. "My Gracie goes off, and she does not come home. Em she is worried, and when Em is worried, my heart cries. So I go to look and I find Gracie's car, and your car, bad man, with the distributor caps missing."

"Distributor caps!" Grace exclaimed.

"Ah, ha!" Dan said, and pointed his finger in the air as if he'd just discovered a new drug.

"Perry," Dan and Grace said at the same time.

"Perry?" Olaf glanced at Grace. She nodded.

Olaf's scowl was sinister. He'd never liked Perry either. In fact, Olaf didn't like anyone who wasn't a Jewel or a relative thereof.

"So you see, Olaf," Dan said, in a perfectly reasonable, doctorlike voice, which was spoiled by the sight of him barefoot and covered in mud. "I had no nefarious designs on your Gracie."

"I only know what I saw. And I think to myself when I find cars and no people—where would my Gracie be? And I wonder about the bad man."

Dan scowled and opened his mouth to protest. Olaf ignored him. Olaf was on a roll. "Then I come here and what do I find? The bad man behaving with inappropriateness to my Gracie. Again."

Olaf stepped forward, and when Grace would have intervened, he silenced her with a look. Olaf had been her teacher, her mentor, her best friend, and her advisor for a very long time. When her father died and bad things began to happen, she had run away, but she had found Olaf. His no-nonsense way of looking at life and saying whatever he thought had soothed her broken heart and calmed her raging soul.

Olaf loved her like the child he never spoke of, and he was not a man to be silenced for any reason—especially when he believed inappropriateness was involved. Sometimes she wished she'd never taught him that word.

Dan shot her a look that plainly shouted, "Help!" But Grace just spread her hands. He was on his own.

Dan watched Grace shrug and turn him over to the monster in the white muscle shirt. This was what happened when you followed your instincts, kicked off your shoes, danced in the mud, and lived a little.

You ended up beaten to a pulp by a masseur.

"Hold on." Dan held his hands out, palms up, toward Olaf. He hoped it was a gesture of surrender, or stop, even in Norwegian. The man stopped. Dan took a deep breath. "I admit, I kissed Grace."

Olaf hissed. Dan wished he'd stop doing that. It was distracting.

"But she kissed me back. Tell him, Grace." She didn't say anything. Dan glanced her way. "Grace?"

She stared at him with an odd expression, as if she couldn't quite figure out what species he was. The look made him as nervous as Olaf's hovering fists. "Grace. Tell him. Don't lie."

Dan suddenly hung a few inches above the ground by his shirt. He'd seen people hanging from their shirts before, usually in *Lethal Weapon* movies, but he'd never actually had the procedure done to him. He doubted anyone but Olaf could manage it.

"Gracie does not lie," Olaf said.

"Of course not," Dan agreed, as if he were talking to an insane person, which he was starting to think Olaf was. "Grace?"

"I kissed him back." She didn't sound happy about it. Both Olaf and Dan frowned.

Olaf released him and Dan rubbed his neck. How was he going to keep Olaf from killing him over the next few weeks, which he must spend with Grace? They were only supposed to be working together, but the way things were going, Dan didn't know how long he'd be able to keep from touching her again—even if touching her wasn't healthy.

Olaf turned his back on Dan as if he weren't there. To tell the truth, that was a bit insulting. Dan was a big guy. Not as big as Olaf, but he could do some damage. If he wanted to. He just didn't want to. But Olaf acted as if he had nothing to fear from Dan Chadwick. Dan sighed. He honestly didn't have a single killer instinct. His instincts had always leaned more toward life. He couldn't help it.

"Gracie, what are you thinking kissing one such as this? Don't you remember what happened the last time?"

The last time? What last time? Dan went still as a mouse, hoping they would forget he was there and keep on talking.

There was no moss on Grace, however. She looked at Dan over Olaf's shoulder, glared at him, then snapped at Olaf. "Of course I remember. This is different."

"How different? He seems the same to me."

"Maybe so. But *I'm* not the same."

Grace stalked by Olaf and headed for the car. "I'll be back in the morning, Doctor." She threw the words over her shoulder, as if she couldn't wait to be gone from here, from him. Maybe she couldn't. "We can work then. My afternoons and early evenings are booked by the tourists."

"Work? Work? Work at what?" Olaf thundered.

Dan kept his mouth shut. Let Grace handle her bodyguard, bodybuilder.

Grace stopped halfway between the car and Dan, and the beam of the headlights showed him every expression on her face. Right now she looked tired and a bit sad.

"Mrs. Cabilla has asked me to help Dr. Chadwick

with his research," she said. "In turn Dr. Chadwick will help me with the hospital administrations."

Olaf let out a stream of guttural gibberish that made Grace flinch, then blush. "There's no cause for that language," she said.

"You understand Norwegian?" Dan couldn't keep the surprise from his voice.

"And Gaelic, French, English, and Ojibwe."

"French?" Dan gritted his teeth. He sounded like a damned parrot.

She reached the car, opened the door and turned, placing her arms along the top of the window, then leaning against it. "I had to take a language in college."

"College?" Surprised again.

"I came, I saw, I dropped out." She got into the car.

Dan glanced at Olaf, who still scowled at him as if he'd just ravished Grace on the ground with the entire world watching. Well almost, but not quite.

"You are not the only one who has a brain, bad man."

Dan ignored what seemed to be his new nickname. Arguing with Olaf felt like banging his head against a brick. No point to either one, and you got a hell of a headache. "What did Grace go to college for?"

"You will have to ask Gracie." *Sniff.* "When you work together."

Then he walked by Dan, bumping him with a shoulder just for the heck of it, got into the car, and slammed the vehicle into reverse.

If Grace's car theory rang true, Olaf should drive

a monster truck. Instead he drove a late 50s model Plymouth Fury, which for some reason seemed just right, though Dan couldn't recall why. What was it about such a car that nagged at his memory?

Dan could see Grace's incredible face through the windshield, her dark eyes fixed on him as she receded down the long tunnel of trees that lined his driveway. Dan felt like a child left at Boy Scout camp in disgrace.

The car disappeared, and the rumble of the engine as it started down the highway back toward town made Dan suddenly remember what nagged him about the Plymouth Fury.

The Fury *was* a monster car. The car that never died. A Stephen King car—Christine, by name. Perhaps there was more to Grace's car theory than he'd given her credit for. In fact, there was a lot more to Grace Lighthorse than Dan could ever have imagined before he'd met her.

Now that he had met her, he planned to spend the next few weeks imagining a whole lot more.

Seven

Being a morning person, Grace awoke with the dawn. This practice annoyed countless people, but she could never figure out why anyone would want to lie in bed right through the most beautiful part of the day.

By the time everyone else in her household stirred, Grace would have taken her walk through town, picked up some coffee and come back to sit on the porch, stitch whatever blanket she was working on at the time—be it quilt or afghan—and watch Lake Illusion come to life.

The vista never changed, but the people did. Sure, some of them were locals, but the tourists spiced up the view, and there were always a few early runners she could watch with bemusement.

"Running?" she murmured. "Bluck!"

Why run through life when you could get where you were going much easier by walking? You'd still get there, more slowly, true, but you'd be able to experience your journey. You could stop and study anything, really *see* the world, rather than pass it by in a blur. If life was a journey, then every day was a new city on your path.

Grace picked up the material she'd been hand-quilting and jabbed her needle into cloth gaily decorated with balloons in primary colors.

Now, she wasn't saying exercise was a bad thing—but hurrying everywhere was. It disturbed Grace to see kids being taught from the ground up to hurry, hurry, hurry. Get there before everyone else. Be the best. Trample those in front of you. You just had to wonder . . . did anyone stop and smell the coffee anymore?

Grace sighed and took a deep drag of her own coffee, first with her nose, then with her mouth. Half the joy in coffee was smelling it first. The dark, heated brew slid down her throat and warmed her from the inside out as she contemplated the sun bursting to life behind the trees outside of town.

One of the reasons she had left Minneapolis and come home was that she just couldn't take the pace of the big city any longer. Especially the pace of the children.

Stress in children concerned Grace. A lot. Kids should run, and jump, and play, sweetly oblivious of the problems awaiting them when they became adults. The problems were still there once they got older—so why get excited ahead of time?

And when sick kids got stressed, that was the worst stress of all, because stress lowered the immune system, and sick kids needed immunity as much as they needed something to hold on to.

So it followed that if a comfort item lowered stress, and lower stress aided the immune system: sick kids needed blankies. She wasn't going to let the naysayers drag her down. Not even a naysayer that kissed as good as—

"Morning!" Dan Chadwick jogged in place on the sidewalk in front of her house. Speak of the naysayer.

I should have figured him for a bright and shiny morning runner.

"Morning," Grace returned. No reason to be rude, even though she wanted to. She'd seen enough of *him* in her dreams.

"You always up this early?" He kept right on jogging, going nowhere.

Her gaze trailed over the tautly muscled legs revealed by his shorts, taking in the miniscule amount of sweat that darkened his maroon half-shirt. These observations, combined with the fact that he could talk without huffing, and nary a puff to be heard, revealed Dr. Dan as a career runner.

Once again, that figured. She wasn't even going to think about the washboard stomach, traced with a light dusting of golden hair revealed by that skimpy shirt. It was just too early in the morning to taste lust on the tongue, so she took a sip of coffee instead.

"I always like to greet the sun," she answered. "And you?"

"I like to get my five miles in before breakfast."

Five miles? Grace rolled her eyes without even trying to hide it. "Overachiever," she mumbled.

"Excuse me?" He probably couldn't hear her over the tromp of his busy, busy feet.

"Nothing. You jogged in from the camp?"

He smiled, happy as a puppy chewing its favorite

dirty sock. If he could pretend that last night's debacle had never happened, so could she. "Yes, from the camp to town and back is a near-perfect five miles."

"Goody." Now that sounded surly, like she was cranky at this hour. And she wasn't—under most circumstances anyway—and with most people. So Grace attempted to be civil, putting down her coffee and not even picking up her quilt block so she could give Dan her full attention. "I've never seen you go by before."

"Never have. Just figured I'd take a different route today."

"Checking up on me, Doc?"

He shrugged. "You never said what time of the morning you'd come by."

"How's right now?"

He stopped tromping in place. "You want to jog back with me?"

She laughed. "I don't think so. Jogging is not something I encourage in myself."

"But it's natural."

"No, walking is natural. Running is something you do to get away from predators."

And I may do it to get away from you later, she thought.

"How are you going to get to the lake?"

"Olaf's car."

"Christine?"

Grace glanced about. They were alone. Had a gear slipped in his brilliant brain? Probably from all that jogging and jiggling. "I'm Grace, Dan."

He grinned and started to stretch—arms over the

head, reaching for the sky, revealing the taut belly, making Grace crazy. Grace yanked her gaze from his stomach, and her sudden fantasy of running her fingers through that soft hair, then pressing her lips to each individual muscle evaporated. She really needed to get a grip.

"I haven't lost my marbles—not yet anyway. I'm talking about Olaf's Fury, which, by the way, makes your car theory seem pretty plausible."

"How so?" She'd always thought Olaf's boat of a car fit him, too, but she wondered why Dr. Dan, the incredible, edible stiff agreed with her.

"It's a Christine car." He came up from a runner's stretch and caught the look of complete blankness on her face. "You know . . . Stephen King? *Christine?* Killer car? Very Olaf."

Down he went again, head reaching for his knee. That had to hurt, but he seemed to like it. Grace's idea of stretching came when she reached for the coffee in the freezer.

Well, that wasn't exactly true. She did yoga when she had time, which was rarely, but yoga never seemed like exercise—more like relaxation and alignment. Grace cracked her neck. Maybe she should dust that videotape off. Just watching Dan made her tense.

"I have no idea what you're talking about," she said. "Except that Stephen King is a writer."

Up came his head, surprise on his face. "You've never read him?"

She shook her head. "Not me. I figured you for the medical journal type."

"I am." He went up on tiptoe, stretching his feet.

"But sometimes I have to read something else. Don't you?"

"I don't have time for fiction." For some reason her voice sounded stiff, snotty. She couldn't believe it. Dan was rubbing off on her.

"Too bad. Reading fiction relaxes me. You might want to try it."

"Do I seem stressed to you?"

"Uh . . . yes."

"I am not!"

He shrugged, beginning to jog in place again. "Maybe you should cut down on the caffeine."

The man had the nerve to preach to her? He lived alone in a broken-down Boy Scout camp, jogged at the crack of dawn, and was afraid of raccoons. She narrowed her eyes. "I don't drink; I don't smoke; I don't do drugs. Touch my coffee and you die."

Incredibly, he laughed. Her blood pressure soared.

"See you soon?" he asked.

Grace walked inside, not bothering to agree or disagree. She had no choice but to see him soon.

The door hadn't closed completely behind Grace when a window on the third floor slammed open with a bang.

"Yoo-hoo, Doctor!"

Dan glanced up to find Em hanging out the third-story window. He raised a hand in greeting, but she waved that off like a fly in front of her nose. "When I wake up in the morning, my gluteous maximus has no feeling."

Before Dan could open his mouth, not that he'd know what to say about her butt falling asleep, the window to the right of hers slipped up and Garnet popped through. "I can't hear out of my left ear."

"You never could, dear," Em pointed out.

"What was that?" Garnet shouted.

Wham! The window on the other side of Em banged skyward. Ruby leaned through the opening. "My corns itch at night."

Laughter drifted from the front door. Dan lowered his gaze. Grace stood behind the screen, the mesh making her look ethereal, even more beautiful than usual. Or maybe it was just because last night he had touched her, kissed her, dreamed of her. When morning came, he could not wait another second to see her face, or hear her voice.

Then he'd annoyed her—though she was cute when she wanted to kick his butt—and now she laughed at him. He just couldn't figure the woman out, or any woman for that matter.

Another window banged open and Dan jumped, yanking his gaze from Grace and up to the fourth story, just in time to see a sheet of water tumbling down. Too late to move, he caught the water right in the face. Someone had taken it out of the ice-cold section of the refrigerator. Dan discovered what it was like to fight for your next breath.

"What is all the shouting at this un-Jesus-ly time of the day? And what are you doing outside my Em's window?"

My Em, my Gracie—did every woman belong to Olaf?

Dan blinked the water out of his eyes. After the

initial shock, the coolness trickling over his heated body didn't feel too bad. He probably looked pretty stupid, but he was used to that. A lifetime of having feet too big, hands too wide, and a head too tall, had let him in for some mighty embarrassing moments. He had just hoped not to look stupid in front of Grace. Too late.

Dan lowered his gaze to the front porch. She was gone. Maybe Lady Luck had been on his side for a change and she had missed the looking stupid part.

"Olaf!" Em scolded, hanging out the window at a dangerous angle so she could look up another story. "What do you think you're doing, throwing water on the doctor like that? He'll never come back."

"That is why I did it, sweet Em. He is a very bad man."

Dan sighed.

"Bad?" Em turned her head and stared down at Dan in confusion. "Well, he is a *doctor.* . . ." She wrinkled her nose. "But he seemed different from the others."

Dan had always been different from the others. But no one he'd known had ever liked that in him. In his world being different was an insult, not a compliment.

"Are you different, Doctor?"

Dan met Em's gaze. Her kind green eyes urged him to tell her all his secrets. "Yeah, I'm different all right."

Olaf snorted, but before he could insult Dan any further, there came a bang, a slam, and a shout: "Olaf! Get your big head back in here!"

Olaf's big head disappeared in a flash and shouts drifted through his window. Dan couldn't understand the argument, probably because it was in an unintelligible mix of languages, but he knew the sound of Grace's voice, even on high volume.

The window slammed shut, causing Dan to flinch, but the Jewels weren't bothered. Perhaps they were *all* a bit deaf.

"Never mind that, dear. Grace has a temper. So does Olaf. They'll scream, and shout, and throw a few things. Then it will all be over and everything will go back to normal."

"Or as normal as we like it around here," Ruby added.

"There's a horrible pike soaked in beer?" shouted Garnet. "Olaf promised he would quit making *luttafisk*. I'm not eating that stuff again."

Dan should run home. *Run, Dan, run.* His clothes no longer felt cool, just wet, and sticky, and kind of . . . He shifted his shoulders and the shirt clung. Kind of yucky. But he couldn't get the idea of Grace shouting and throwing things out of his head. A temper seemed so . . . so . . . so un-Grace.

Something thudded against the upstairs wall. Dan scowled. "He wouldn't hurt her, would he?"

"Bite your tongue, young man. Olaf never laid a hand on a woman in his life."

"Now, Em, that's not true," Ruby corrected. Dan started for the front door. "He lays hands on women every day when he massages them."

Dan stopped and sighed. He was getting a headache. "What's Grace so mad about anyway?"

"Why, you, Doctor. What else is there?"

"Me?" What had he done now?

"Olaf threw water on you."

Dan winced. Grace had seen that. Lady Luck had never been kind to him before, why would she start now?

"That was very discourteous," Em continued. "Although in Olaf's defense, he loves Grace to the very corners of his huge heart."

Dan found the image of Olaf loving Grace with all his heart very disquieting. No wonder Olaf had thrown a fit upon finding Dan and Grace in the mud last night. Dan was lucky to be alive.

Slam! Bang! Bump! echoed from the upstairs room. Em grinned, as if their behavior were just the cutest thing she'd ever seen. "She's furious. You may as well go home and get cleaned up. Those two will be awhile."

Dan nodded, bemused. In his family one would never deign to shout. And to throw things? So inappropriate. So *bourgeois*. No one raised their voice; no one swore beyond a polite "damn." And no one seemed to give a damn about anyone else either. At least passion lived in this house.

Crash.

"Oh, dear, that sounded like glass," Em murmured.

A lot of passion, Dan amended.

He trotted back down the sidewalk, but Em called, "Come for dinner tonight. I insist."

Glancing over his shoulder, Dan found the ladies waving "bye-bye," except for Em, because it hurt when she did that. The sight was so sweet he waved back, and in doing so, discovered he'd agreed to dinner without saying a single word.

Grace arrived at the old Boy Scout camp on Lake Illusion before 9 A.M. She felt ever so much better after throwing a few things at Olaf. After she'd gotten that out, she explained to him that though he might not like Dan Chadwick, that was just tough tootsies. Grace had to work with the man for the next several weeks or forfeit Project Hope. She was not about to do that for anyone, or anything. After much mumbling, grumbling, and shouting, Olaf agreed to keep his big nose out of things—as much as he was able to, at least.

Grace had an Irish temper, which her mother always insisted she'd gotten from her great-granny, the flame-haired witch. Grace's father had never understood her volatile nature; her paternal grandparents had been horrified.

Stoicism in the face of adversity was their way. A Lighthorse did not scream and shout. Obviously they had never seen their son in court. But then Joseph Lighthorse had always danced to his own drum, and to hell with everyone else. Funny, but when Grace did the same dance, he had not found it half as admirable as his own.

What no one but Em had ever understood was that Grace did not *choose* to be this way. This was the way she was.

Most days found Grace calm, cool, and competent. But on others the top of her head felt ready to explode, and if she didn't shout or throw something, her brains would be on the outside instead of in. Those days seemed to be on the upswing with Dan in town.

Grace knocked on the door of the cabin. Several moments later she still stood on the porch alone. Since Dan's car remained at Mrs. Cabilla's, along with her own, Grace couldn't tell if he was home or not. But where could he be? She didn't have time to wait around. She had a noon appointment.

With a shrug, Grace tried the door. It swung open with a loud squeak. Seemed Dr. Dan hadn't been keeping up on the maintenance at Camp Illusion.

Grace stepped inside. A feeling of otherworldliness swept over her at the sight of a full laboratory set up within the log cabin. Once upon a time this place had been the mess hall and kitchen, which made the building the largest of any other at camp. The shoulder-high windows were all shut, keeping out the breeze. But the room wasn't unpleasant; in fact the temperature was perfect.

Grace sniffed the air and caught just a trace of artificial coolness, a scent like iron in ice-cold water. Dr. Dan had air-conditioning, courtesy of Mrs. Cabilla no doubt. He didn't have the air on full blast, but still it must cost a bundle to cool this barn. She had an image of money burning on a campfire. *Her* money.

"This can't be very sterile," she observed.

"Actually, it is."

Grace jumped right out of her skin at the sound of Dan's voice. He leaned in the doorway of what had once been the kitchen, drying his hands on a towel. He looked good enough to eat, too. His hair still damp from his shower, looked darker and curlier than usual. His khaki pants and blue, short-sleeved dress shirt, looked like they had been washed but not ironed. He got several points for being rumpled.

He walked toward her. Grace liked to watch him walk. Dan might be large, but he moved lightly enough on his feet. Lighter than Olaf anyway, which wasn't saying much. Olaf had flat feet.

Grace's gaze went to Dan's feet. They were bare. She gave him three points for that. Not only were they bare, but very, very nice. As nice as the rest of him—and she was in a position to know exceptional body parts when she saw them.

"Grace?"

She glanced at his face. He'd been talking to her while she stared at his feet. Jeez, she was never going to be able to work with this guy if she couldn't stop staring at every bare part of his body. What was wrong with her?

"Yes?"

Luckily, he didn't seem to notice her preoccupation as he was interested in talking about his work. "I was explaining that as long as we have sterile fields and hands, the work is safe."

Grace made a noncommittal sound. *Whatever.* "Temperature is nice in here. Must be a bear to air-condition with that ceiling and all those windows, but then I suppose *you* don't get the bills."

The intent, almost happy gaze he'd turned upon her while explaining his work became a frown. "I don't spend money needlessly. The work needs to be kept at a constant temperature or I wouldn't bother with artificial cooling."

He said "the work" like other people said "the pope" or "the attorney general." Grace sighed. Or like she said "Project Hope." She was being prickly and had no cause. She'd agreed to help the man and help him she would. For three weeks.

"What would you like me to do?"

"Right now, come with me." He spun on his heel and headed back toward the kitchen without bothering to see if she followed. Obviously he expected her to do so without question.

Grace gritted her teeth and did just that. No sense getting in an argument over the first order he gave her. She'd already had a great big argument today, and while it had felt wonderful at the time to get all the tension on the outside instead of in, right now she had no desire to exhaust herself any further with emotions and temper.

Dan disappeared through the open doorway. Grace followed and discovered a kitchen gleaming with silver countertops and cabinets. The place was spotless. Had Dan done this, or did he have a maid? A maid would really annoy her.

A door slammed at the back of the cabin, and Grace hustled through the kitchen in time to see Dan crossing the small bit of yard between the main building and a smaller cabin. She hurried across, catching the door as he slipped inside.

Hesitating there, she took stock of the room. While the lab had been spotless, and organized in a near-military fashion, this place had an absent-minded professor quality—books jumbled on every available surface, papers poured across the floor, clothes stuffed into a free-standing closet.

A king-sized bed dominated the cabin. He must need a big bed—just look at him—but the way the thing consumed the room . . . well, it made Grace nervous. Especially since Dan stared at her from the other side of the bed as if waiting for her to meet him in the middle. She continued to hover by the door.

"Listen to this." Dan pushed a button on the answering machine, which sat between two precarious towers of books atop the nightstand. Perry's voice filled the cabin and Grace couldn't stop herself from scowling.

"Don't bother to come looking for me, Chadwick. Mrs. Cabilla has given me leave and I've already left. You and Miss Lighthorse are on your own. Play nice. And your distributor caps are in the lake." He hung up snickering, and Dan jabbed the erase button with a curse.

"What do you make of that?" he asked. "Think the guy has finally gone to the dark side?"

"He didn't have far to travel if he did. Weasel spirit."

Dan laughed. The sound was so infectious, Grace laughed, too. "I figured it was just me who thought he looked like a weasel," he said.

"How could it be just you when the guy *does* look like a weasel? I think his aura would be muddy gray." She wrinkled her nose. "That shade indicates a sneaky person."

"Aura?" Dan's smile died. "You're kidding, right?"

"Why would I kid about something like that?"

"You see auras?"

"Well, I don't see floating colored clouds, though I've heard some people do. The aura is an energy field that surrounds every living thing. I feel things about people, and for me, feelings have colors."

He didn't look convinced, but what did she care? There was no use trying to explain feelings to people. Especially people like him.

"If Perry is gray, what am I?"

She caught a glimpse of a vulnerable little boy within those midnight eyes. A little boy who wanted her to tell him he was gold. Gold was very good.

Grace refused to tell him what he really was, because passion was red, awareness orange, and those little silver twinkles meant fertility.

She crimped her lips together and shook her head, and the little boy fled. Dr. Chadwick came back. He was kind of gray, too, but a shade of gray that meant he left no job undone.

"This is serious work here." Dan's voice had gone stuffy again. "I need serious help."

Damn, she was good. The guy needed to loosen up, or at least let go of that gray part of himself once in awhile. Maybe a few rounds with Olaf would help Dan more than it had helped her, but she doubted Dan would see it that way.

"I am serious. Just because you can't see something doesn't mean it isn't there. Do you see the air you breathe? Do you see love? Do you see the wind? No wonder you can't find a cure. You need to look past the nose on your face."

"That's what Mrs. Cabilla said."

"She was right."

He looked at her for a long time, and while his eyes looked storm-tossed, his voice, when he spoke, was as calm as a lake 'round about midnight.

"We should get back to the lab. I already called the service station in town, told them about the distributor cap theft at Mrs. Cabilla's, and asked them to drive the cars home for us once they've fixed them."

Grace had to wonder if he'd heard a thing she'd said. The man was infuriating. "Such service," she mocked. "Are you buying? Or is this on Mrs. Cabilla?"

He didn't take the bait. Dan was a very hard man to rile. From the muscle working in his jaw, he also looked to be a prime candidate for an ulcer. "Nope," he said. "It's on Perry."

"You think so?"

Dan looked her straight in the eye. "I know so."

Grace tilted her head and stared right back. She liked what she saw. Perry didn't stand a chance.

Eight

They were on their own—for three weeks. No Perry, no Mrs. Cabilla. Just Dan and Grace, in the lab. Would he live through it? Or self-detonate from repressed lust and aggravated annoyance? Grace pushed his buttons as no one else ever had. Had she brought up that aura stuff just to see what he'd do? Nah, sensing auras was very Grace.

He stared at her over the wide expanse of his bed. She'd twisted her hair into one of those braids that started at the center of her forehead, wiggled over the crown, and squiggled all the way down her back. *Fancy.* He'd like to watch her do that—preferably naked, right here on this bed.

Dan gave himself a good mind-cursing. He would never make it through the next few weeks without dreaming of her—of touching her, kissing her, wanting her. Inappropriate things to feel for his research assistant—especially one with a partner who wanted to break him in half just for breathing.

Dan soothed his conscience with the fact that he hadn't hired her; she'd been foisted upon him. He wasn't paying her, so she wasn't really an employee. True enough, but a sense of impropriety remained—and with it just a twinge of the forbidden that had always excited him. "A little rebellion problem," as his mother liked to call it.

While a child, temptation had always called to Dan louder than most. He'd rarely been able to resist—even though he quickly learned that he always got caught, embarrassed, and punished. Yet temptation continued to beckon to his rebellious soul. Right now temptation's name was Grace.

Dan dragged his gaze from her face and glanced at his watch. He stared, then blinked. The time remained the same. A glance at the bedside clock revealed the same time, and he started around the bed.

He'd been daydreaming in here for a quarter of an hour. He never did that. He couldn't do that and keep his research alive. There were too many pots boiling on his stove to daydream, but obviously the tendency to daydream increased with the scent of Grace on the wind.

He motored around the bed and headed for the door, intending to brush by her. Instead, being Dan, he bumped into her.

She stumbled a bit and he caught her elbows. She glanced into his face. He completely forgot what was cooking in the lab as things heated up considerably in his cabin. Especially him.

His hands slid beneath the short sleeves of her loose-fitting, neon-orange jumpsuit. Only Grace could wear such a thing and make the outfit look like a ten-thousand-dollar wedding gown instead of prison attire. His thumbs caressed inside of her arm, sliding across the softest skin he'd ever known.

She shuddered at his stroke and tried to pull away. Dan took a deep breath and tasted Grace on his tongue without even trying. His body kicked into the next dimension, just as the smoke alarm went off in the lab.

Dan picked Grace up and set her aside, then ran toward the blare of sound. He burst through the back door, skidded through the kitchen and came to a dead stop inside the laboratory. Grace thumped into his back.

"Umph," she said. "What is it?"

He grunted and approached a boiling cauldron on a hot plate. He'd purposely put the hot plate beneath the smoke alarm to keep accidents to a minimum in his lab made of wood. Not that he'd ever burned a place down—not yet anyway. To be honest, he'd never forgotten an experiment before, but then he'd never had Grace in his bedroom before either.

"Can you make that noise stop?" Grace asked in a tight voice.

Dan glanced over his shoulder to find her wincing at the volume of sound, hands over her ears, shoulders hunched. She looked like she was in pain, and he hurriedly removed his experiment from the hot plate and walked away, waving his free hand through the steam to disperse the heat. A few seconds later, the alarm squawked one last time and went silent.

Dan was already intent upon what was in the pan. He'd meant for the concoction to boil to just that point; the experiment wasn't ruined, but it didn't yield anything new either. His sigh came from the depths of his disappointed soul.

"What's the matter?"

The sound of Grace's voice made Dan start. He just wasn't used to people hanging around in the lab, and Grace moved so quietly she'd snuck up on him. Not that he'd completely forgotten she was there—how could he?—but he'd spaced out of this world for a moment.

Dan set the pan back on the counter, put his hands on the edge, and let his head fall between his shoulders. "Nothing's the matter."

"Is the experiment ruined?"

"No."

"Then why the face?"

He straightened. "What face?"

"This one." Grace pulled her features into an exaggerated version of despair.

Dan laughed, surprising himself. She made him laugh in times of trouble. No one ever had before. "I didn't look like that," he said, still laughing because she was still making the face.

She stopped. "How would you know? I was the one doing the looking."

Silence fell between them. They'd both been doing a lot of looking—and a lot of touching. Dan wanted to do a lot more. From the look on her face, so did Grace.

She turned away, walking toward the bank of windows that overlooked the lake, and staring through them as if she could find answers out there to her greatest dilemma. Dan wished answers were that easy to find. If they were, he'd look out those windows a whole lot more.

"This has got to stop," she said, still looking at the lake.

"What?"

"All the looking, and the touching, and the kissing."

"Why?" He sounded like an instructional tape on the best way to write a newspaper article—who, what, when, where, why and how—if you needed those questions asked, then Dan was your man.

"We'll never get anything done if we keep drooling all over each other."

Dan did not drool, but he got her point. "Maybe we should just sleep together and get it out of our systems."

That surprised a bark of laughter from Grace. "Spoken like a true man."

Dan straightened. No one had ever called him a true man before, though her words hadn't sounded like a compliment.

Grace turned. "I don't think so, Dan."

His shoulders sagged again. "Why not?" Sounded like a great idea to him.

"Because this"—she moved her slim, long-fingered, naked hands about in a dance that aroused him right then and there—"this doesn't feel like something that would burn out in one session to me. Does it to you?"

He was silent for a long moment. Truth or dare? He couldn't lie about this. He couldn't lie about much of anything. "No."

"So instead of working we'd be . . ." She shrugged. "You know."

"And that would be bad?"

"Yes. I don't sleep with the enemy, Dan."

"I'm not the enemy."

"Yes, you are. We both want the same thing—the Cabilla Grant. I'm not giving it up. Are you?"

"No."

"Then let's get started." She stepped toward the worktable.

He put a hand out to stop her. "How do I know you won't sabotage my work?"

She looked at him as if he were the biggest idiot on the planet. Grace could make him feel like that as easily as she could make him feel like the coolest guy on campus.

Women, he thought. Or maybe just *Grace.*

"Why would I sabotage your work? If we find a cure, you're out of my hair. If I screw you up, and Mrs. Cabilla finds out, I'm out on my butt. I'd be better off helping you. Besides . . ." She sighed. "I really could use some help with those stiffs at the hospital." She looked him up and down. Even though the look was cool, Dan went hot. "I think you talk their language in your sleep."

"Want to find out?"

"Dan!" She smiled at him like he'd just discovered penicillin. "You made a joke."

Not really, but if making a joke caused her to smile like that, he was willing to play along.

"There's a first time for everything," he said.

Grace spent the rest of the morning typing the results of Dan's experiments into a computer program. Seemed Dan could do many things, but typing was not one of them.

"My fingers are too big. They hit two keys at once sometimes."

His face reddened as if that were his fault—and a major fault at that. Grace looked at her own bird-fingers, as Olaf always called them, and wished she had such problems. In her business, big hands were a good thing.

Grace shrugged. "My father always said typing was a marketable skill. He was big on marketable skills. He had me pecking away at his office from the day I knew my letters."

"You must be pretty good."

"Eighty-five words a minute."

He gaped. "You could get a pretty good job doing that."

Her smile at his comical expression of amazement froze at the accidental insult of his words. "I *have* a pretty good job, without sitting on my butt and doing other people's grunt work."

"Sorry," he mumbled. "This wasn't my idea, if you'll recall."

"I know." She put out her hand. "Just give me the stuff and show me what you want me to do with it."

In large but extraordinarily neat handwriting, Dan had recorded every little thing. So Grace typed every little thing into a program Dan had created for just that purpose. She had no idea what any of it meant, but she didn't need to. She just needed to type, like any good grunt. The data would be collated once she'd entered everything—or so he said.

Grace was pretty impressed—with the program and with Dan's handwriting. Un-doctor man strikes again.

Coming to the end of a page, Grace glanced at her watch and then at Dan. He was bent over a beaker, mumbling like a madman. He'd been doing that for the past hour and a half—ever since she'd asked him what paronychial infection was, and he'd told her, in med-speak.

Her mind whirred; her eyes rolled back in her head. She had no idea what he was talking about, and when his voice had disintegrated into mumbles, she'd just walked away, leaving him in his own little universe. He'd never noticed she was gone.

No wonder he liked to work alone. He sounded like a Saturday afternoon matinee monster when he mumbled like that. She'd just have to look up paronychial infection later—if she could manage to read through the definition without falling asleep.

She pushed back her chair. Time to go home.

"Dan?"

Grunt.

"I have to go."

Grunt.

"I'll be back tomorrow morning."

Nothing.

Grace picked up the keys to Olaf's car and went to the door. "The conversation has been enlightening; the company charming."

He held up one finger, as if asking her to wait one minute. Grace did. When his finger was still up in the air four minutes later, she shook her head and left. But she did so with a smile. Unfortunately, she found the absentminded professor thing kind of cute.

Five hours later, the smile had died along with her energy. Grace sat on her front porch and flapped a weak hand at her last customer of the day. She was beat. All she wanted to do was take a tepid shower, put on her jammies, and help the Jewels piece together a quilt in the workroom. Maybe play some music, have a fruit and yogurt smoothie for dinner.

Her eyes drifted closed, her head fell back, her legs stretched out in front of her. She imagined the thick, white yogurt blended with blueberries and bananas, cooling her heated tongue, sliding down her parched throat, soothing her empty stomach.

A car door slammed and absently Grace dismissed the sound as her last customer belatedly leaving. She went back to the fruit smoothie fantasy with a lick of her lips. She could almost taste the froth that floated on the top of the drink; the bubbles would burst upon her tongue with a mere hint of flavor, then disappear. As if in protest, her stomach rumbled, and she rubbed her palm over her belly in a circular motion until it calmed.

Summer heat hung on the air and with a sigh, Grace popped open the next three buttons on her jumpsuit, down to where the clasp would be on a front-clasp bra—if she wore a bra. She'd never seen the point of wasting her money in the training-bra section at Sears.

Dusk marked her second-favorite time of the day. Work was done and play about to begin. The night was hers and she could hardly wait.

A breeze drifted across Lake Illusion, cooling the beads of sweat upon her bare chest, then picking up a stray lock of hair that had escaped from her French braid. The strand tickled her nose and she giggled, then ran fingertips down her collarbone and spread the droplets into nothing.

Someone choked; glass shattered, and Grace leapt to her feet.

Dan Chadwick stood at the base of her porch steps, a broken bottle at his feet. Red wine soaked into the dirt and the cement, ran down his bare shins and beaded upon his canoe-sized tennis shoes.

He looked up, and in his eyes Grace saw a heat that had nothing to do with embarrassment. It was then that she understood the car door she'd heard had been his, and he'd been watching her all along. Watching her imagine an orgasmic meal, watching her open her shirt, watching her touch herself and sigh.

Grace swallowed a scalding lump at the base of her throat, but she could not break the pull of his gaze, even if she'd wanted to.

The breeze picked up again but could do little to dispel the heat that flushed over her. The scent of the wine, rich and red, rose on the steamy afternoon, wrapping about her, making her ache. She took a step toward him and he shook his head.

"The glass," he murmured, then stepped over the mess and up the steps.

He stood too close, and she didn't care. She wanted those big hands on her. She wanted them on her now.

She watched him raise his hand and her eyes

drifted closed, her head drifted back, revealing the line of her throat, opening her blouse to the swell of her breasts—what swell there was.

Then he touched her, a single feather-light flick across her cheek as he pushed the stray lock of hair behind her ear. She waited for his kiss. His lips pressed to her brow. Her eyes opened, confused, as he stepped back and away from her, staring at the door.

Grace turned. Olaf scowled. "Button self, Gracie. Can I not leave you for a moment and you are kissing very bad men?"

"Go away, Olaf. You act like I'm a nymphomaniac."

"Nymph? Perhaps. Maniac? That would be *him.*" Olaf sniffed at Dan, who just shrugged. "Why is he here anyway? Did you not see him enough while you were *working*?"

She'd seen him, but he had not really seen her. Still, why was he here? And with wine? Grace glanced at the mess on the sidewalk. Make that without wine?

"Em invited me to dinner," Dan said.

"What?" Grace squeaked—her jammie-and-smoothie fantasy evaporating on the night breeze.

Olaf cursed in Norwegian. Em sailed out the front door, dressed in her Cleopatra, Queen of the Nile costume. Dan looked back and forth between the two of them. Grace groaned and sat back in her chair.

It was going to be a very long night.

* * *

Dan swept the sidewalk clear of glass and used the hose hooked to the front of the house to spray the cement and his legs. What was it about Grace that turned him into a walking klutz?

That wasn't fair—he'd been a klutz long before he met Grace. It just hurt more when she saw his failings. Grace was so . . . so . . . so Grace. Next to her he was an oaf, and he needed to remember that.

He had come out of the zone to find Grace gone. Long gone to be exact—it was nearly dinnertime before he came back to earth. His mother would say he was rude not to have said good-bye, shown Grace out, thanked her for her trouble, blah, blah, blah. Of course his mother probably wouldn't have let Grace Lighthorse into her house. His mother was the queen of rude, which was why she felt it her duty to point out rudeness in others.

The screen door popped open and Olaf lumbered out. Dan also needed to remember that Olaf loved Grace to the corners of his huge heart, and if Dan screwed up, Olaf might just use his huge fists on Dan's face.

Dan nodded. "Sorry about the mess."

Olaf's lip curled into a snarl. So much for apologies.

Dan climbed the porch steps only to find his entrance blocked. He was not going to get into a shoving match with Olaf. Not only would he lose, he'd most likely end up looking stupid again. Once a day was enough for him, thank you.

"Pardon me?" he tried.

"I will not pardon you. Touching Gracie is forbidden, bad man."

"To you, too?" Dan couldn't help it; it just slipped out. He watched Olaf's face turn crimson, and waited to die.

"Only a man such as you would think such a thing. Gracie is like my baby—the baby I lost long ago in my land of light. I once watched her cry over another such as you, and I did nothing because Gracie asked me not to. This time I will break you . . ." Olaf raised his fists in front of Dan's face and made a snapping motion to illustrate, even though Dan had already gotten the point. "Like this. I will tear off your head and spit in your neck."

"Graphic image," Dan murmured. Olaf had to be descended from Vikings—perhaps only a generation back.

"Even Gracie will not stop me. So watch what you do, bad man, because I will be watching you."

He bumped his shoulder against Dan's in what was becoming a familiar gesture between the two of them—almost as good as a handshake. Dan's footing slipped but he managed to stay on his feet. The guy *was* going to kill him if he stepped out of line.

"Dan?" Grace stood in the doorway, a slight smile on her face.

She looked the same as when he'd watched her on the porch, except she'd buttoned her jumpsuit. Too late, because he'd already seen that there was just Grace beneath the neon light. Would his palms forever itch with the need to slip inside and discover the curve of her rib cage beneath the swell of her breast?

"Yep," he said, to no one in particular.

"Dinner," Grace said and opened the screen.

As her scent mixed with the remnants of wine, Dan admitted to himself that for Grace, death just might be worth a single night in her arms.

THE PUBLISHERS OF ZEBRA BOUQUET

are making this special offer to lovers of contemporary romances to introduce this exciting new line of novels. Zebras Bouquet Romances have been praised by critics and authors alike as being of the highest quality and best written romantic fiction available today.

EACH FULL-LENGTH NOVEL

has been written by authors you know and love as well as by up-and-coming writers that you'll only find with Zebra Bouquet. We'll bring you the newest novels by world famous authors like Vanessa Grant, Judy Gill, Ann Josephson and award winning Suzanne Barrett and Leigh Greenwood—to name just a few. Zebra Bouquet's editors have selected only the very best and highest quality romances for up-and-coming publications under the Bouquet banner.

YOU'LL BE TREATED

to tales of star-crossed lovers in glamourous settings that are sure to captivate you. These stories will keep you enthralled to the very happy end.

4 FREE NOVELS
As a way to introduce you to these terrific romances, the publishers of Bouquet are offering Zebra Romance readers Four Free Bouquet novels. They are yours for the asking with no obligation to buy a single book. Read them at your leisure. We are sure that after you've read these introductory books you'll want more! (If you do not wish to receive any further Bouquet novels, simply write "cancel" on the invoice and return to us within 10 days.)

SAVE 35% WITH HOME DELIVERY
Each month you'll receive four just-published Bouquet romances. We'll ship them to you as soon as they are printed (you may even get them before the bookstores). You'll have 10 days to preview these exciting novels for Free. If you decide to keep them, you'll be billed the special preferred home subscription price of just $3.20 per book; a total of just $12.80 — that's a savings of over 35% off the cover. If for any reason you are not satisfied simply return the novels for full credit, no questions asked. You'll never have to purchase a minimum number of books and you may cancel your subscription at any time.

A ZEBRA BOUQUET ROMANCE

The Right Choice
KARYN LANGHORN

A ZEBRA BOUQUET ROMANCE $3.99

Worth The Wait
KATHRYN ATTALLA

A ZEBRA BOUQUET ROMANCE

The Men of Sugar Mountain
Two Hearts
VIVIAN LEIBER

A ZEBRA BOUQUET ROMANCE

Love In Bloom
MICHAELA CALLAN

GET STARTED TODAY –
NO RISK AND NO OBLIGATION

To get your introductory gift of 4 Free Bouquet Romances fill out and mail the enclosed Free Book Certificate today. We'll ship your free books as soon as we receive this information. Remember that you are under no obligation. This is a risk-free offer from the publishers of Zebra Bouquet Romances.

Call us TOLL FREE at 1-888-345-BOOK
Visit our website at www.kensingtonbooks.com

FREE BOOK CERTIFICATE

YES! I would like to take you up on your offer. Please send me 4 Free Bouquet Romance Novels as my introductory gift. I understand that unless I tell you otherwise, I will then receive the 4 newest Bouquet novels to preview each month FREE for 10 days. If I decide to keep them I'll pay the preferred home subscriber's price of just $3.20 each (a total of only $12.80) plus $1.50 for shipping and handling. That's a savings of over 35% off the cover price. I understand that I may return any shipment for full credit–no questions asked–and I may cancel this subscription at any time with no obligation. Regardless of what I decide to do, the 4 Free Introductory Novels are mine to keep as Bouquet's gift.

BN110A

Name _____

Address _____

City _____ State _____ Zip _____

Telephone ( ) _____

Signature _____

(If under 18, parent or guardian must sign.)

Orders subject to acceptance by Zebra Home Subscription Service. Terms and Prices subject to change.

Offer valid only in the U.S.

If this response card is missing,
call us at 1-888-345-BOOK.

Be sure to visit our website at
www.kensingtonbooks.com

BOUQUET ROMANCES
Zebra Home Subscription Service, Inc.
P.O. Box 5214
Clifton NJ 07015-5214

Nine

"Olaf won't be joining us?" Dan followed Grace into the house. "He have a hot date?"

"Olaf?" Grace laughed. "No. He tells me he loves someone with all his heart, and he'll have no one but her, but she won't have him. I find that hard to believe. He's such a sweet man."

"Sweet? Olaf? We're talking about your partner? The man who wants to kill me?"

"He doesn't want to kill you."

"Yes," Dan said. "He does."

Grace stopped at the foot of the stairs leading up to the second floor offices. She turned with her hand on the newel post. "I told him this morning that you and I were conducting business, and he should leave you alone. Did he threaten you again?"

Dan thought of the argument he'd overheard that morning—the shouts, the thumps, the breaking glass. He didn't want to be responsible for making such a thing happen again, even to Olaf. "No, no threats. Everything's peachy."

Grace narrowed her eyes. "You are a terrible liar, Daniel Chadwick."

"And that would be a bad thing?"

Her lips twitched with a smile she did not allow to bloom before she headed up another flight of stairs. Dan got to follow. He liked following Grace.

As they gained the landing, the sound of arguing Jewels brought an exasperated sigh from Grace. "We'd better hurry up before they start throwing the crockery." She picked up her pace.

"Is that where you get it from?"

"Yes," she said curtly.

They reached a small dining room off the kitchen, which had been added in a renovation. There seemed to be very few doors in the house; huge archways led from the halls into the rooms proper, which gave each floor an airy, open feeling that Dan liked.

Em placed serving bowls in the center of the table. He had to admit the Cleopatra getup became her. The gold sheath complimented her still-slim figure, and the exotic eye makeup, which must have taken hours, made her green eyes glow and her skin shine pale as cream.

The other two had not dressed up—as historical figures at any rate. Instead, they wore flowing, brightly colored dresses, possibly mumus, with matching flowers tucked into their hair. The place had the air of a party, spoiled only by the cutlery joust taking place at the head of the table between Ruby and Garnet.

"Stop that!" Grace ordered. "You'll put out an eye. Or at the very least get a puncture wound like last time."

The two women ignored her, continuing to growl and mumble, fake and jab.

With another exasperated sigh, Grace stepped forward and gingerly de-forked the pair, as if dealing with two very dangerous women. Em raised a perfectly painted eyebrow in Dan's direction and went into the kitchen. Dan just stood in the doorway feeling out of place. Since he usually was, the feeling came as no surprise.

Amazing smells wafted toward Dan, and his stomach growled, then contracted so painfully he got dizzy. He'd forgotten to eat again. That really had to stop.

"What are you two fighting about this time?" Grace sounded weary.

"*She* thought we needed to serve a dead thing for dinner," Ruby accused. Dan's stomach stopped growling.

"She wants to feed the nice young doctor rabbit food."

"Well, *she'd* feed him the rabbit if I let her."

"I do not make a habit of petting birds." Garnet gave Grace a wounded look. "Grace made me stop, though I still don't understand why. The birds loved me and I loved them."

"That's not what I said," Ruby shouted. "She never hears anything right."

"Never mind, Aunt Ruby." Grace turned to her other aunt, who still looked confused. "Birds have germs, Aunt Garnet. You can't bring wild ones into the house. It isn't safe for us or fair to them."

"She didn't want to *pet* them; she wanted to *eat* them. Cannibal."

"What did she call me?" Garnet's hands clenched into fists.

Grace stepped between them. "Now, auntie, we have a guest. Can you get the water?"

Garnet still wanted to belt her sister, Dan could see it in her eyes. Instead she spun on her heel and marched into the kitchen with Em.

Ruby snorted. "If I didn't watch her every minute she'd sneak dead animals onto the table."

"I can hardly wait for dinner," Dan murmured.

"Ruby's an avid vegetarian," Grace explained. "And she does most of the cooking."

"Which makes you all vegetarians?"

"Except for Garnet," Ruby said. "She sneaks out to eat the dead on a bun."

Dan's craving for a bacon cheeseburger died right there.

"Never mind that now," Grace soothed. "Dr. Chadwick is hungry."

Ruby looked Dan up and down. "I bet he's hungry a lot."

Dan, accustomed to being looked upon as different because of his size, if not his strange choice of professions, merely shrugged and remained silent.

Then Em walked in and laced her arm through his. "I do so like a great, big man. They make me feel small and protected." She tugged on his arm and led him toward the table. "You can sit next to me, Doctor. You're my special guest." She shot a glare at Ruby.

Ruby sniffed. "I didn't invite him. Since when do you like doctors?"

"Since I met this one." Em beamed at Dan.

For some reason Dan's usual stiffness around people evaporated around Em. After a few moments in her company he even stopped staring at the cobra headdress that rose up between her eyes.

Em regaled him with five husbands' worth of adventures. She had loved; she had hated; she had traveled; she had lived. Dan was mesmerized. The bowls of food kept coming; Dan kept helping himself and eating. He had to admit that though there wasn't a single dead thing in the bunch, the meal was wonderful.

"And then my fourth husband, or was it my fifth?" Em glanced at Grace, who shrugged and took more caramelized carrots. "Doesn't matter. He took me to Hong Kong, and we brought back this lovely cloth with gold woven right through. Remember, sisters?"

Garnet and Ruby nodded, continuing to eat and glare at each other. Luckily no more arguments or fork fights had broken out.

"We made a crazy quilt and took first prize in a contest sponsored by one of the quilting magazines."

"Three thousand dollars," Grace put in. "Start-up money for their business."

Dan nodded. With the resurgence of interest in history and things made the old-fashioned way, as well as an upswing in mail-order sales and the Internet, he thought the Jewels were on to something with Quilts to Order.

Ruby began to clear the table. "Would you like dessert, Doctor?" She had become friendlier and friendlier the more he ate and ate.

"Call me Dan," he said automatically. Doctor this, doctor that. Drove him nuts.

"Dan." She beamed at him like he'd just said

something so darn cute. Dan wasn't used to being looked at like that. He liked it. "I made cherry cobbler. No eggs, soy milk."

Garnet made a face behind her sister's back.

"Uh . . ." Dan hesitated, then thought of how wonderful the entire vegetarian meal had been. "Sure," he said and earned a smile from everyone but Garnet.

The Jewels bustled into the kitchen. Dan glanced at Grace, and, as usual, discovered he didn't want to look at anything else. "Thank you for dinner. It was wonderful."

"You think? A lot of people would have been asking, 'Where's the meat?' "

"How rude." His mother would have been one of them.

"Yes, isn't it?" She reached over and put her hand atop his, where it lay on the table. "Thank you for being so sweet to my aunts. Not everyone is."

Dan frowned. "Who?"

"Now you look and sound like Olaf. 'Who dares to be inappropriate to my Jewels?' "

"Well, who dares?"

"To be honest, since we moved to Lake Illusion last spring, folks have been pretty nice."

"People weren't nice where you used to live?"

"In Minneapolis there were so many people that most were indifferent."

"And before that?"

The smile she'd turned on him faded. "Before that people were less nice."

"You mean in your hometown? I don't understand."

"It might have been my hometown, but I never belonged there. That's why I didn't go back. Home has always been wherever my aunts are. And now Olaf, too. A place where I feel comfortable, safe, and needed."

"Lake Illusion?"

"Right now, yes, Lake Illusion."

A companionable silence settled between them. He understood what she meant about home being a state of mind and not a place. He felt the same way. In fact, he felt at home right here.

The comforting sounds of the Jewels scraping plates and loading the dishwasher were music to Dan, who usually ate alone in the midst of a great big silence. Sometimes being alone was not all it was cracked up to be—even though he'd always told himself he preferred it. When you were alone you had no one to disappoint but yourself.

Grace sat back and her hand went with her, leaving Dan empty and cold. He clenched his fingers into a fist to keep from entreating her return. Afraid she'd get up and help the Jewels in the kitchen, his mind searched for a topic of conversation to keep her at the table with him.

"You never did tell me what you went to college to be, once upon a time."

Her face froze and Dan cursed himself for an idiot. He wanted to take the question back, but it was too late. Of all the possible topics of conversation, trust him to pick the wrong one.

"I was going to be a lawyer," she said.

"Huh?" *Excellent comeback, Dan,* his mind taunted.

"Actually I pursued a degree in history. It didn't take long before I'd had enough."

"Don't feel bad, a lot of students can't handle the pressure or the classes. It's nothing to be ashamed of."

"That wasn't why I stopped. I was number one in my class, and at the time, pressure was like a drug to me. Until my father died, and I saw what stress could do to a person."

"How did your father die?"

"Stress-related coronary. He was a workaholic. It killed him—plain and simple."

"So you dropped out of college because of that?"

"I dropped out before that."

"Why?"

"People took one look at me and thought 'flake' or worse."

Dan's cheeks burned. He'd done exactly that. "Couldn't you have played the game long enough to get your degree?"

"I'm not good at games. I could change the way I dressed, cut my hair, wear shoes every damn day, but I can't change my face. My skin is this color, my eyes are, too. My name is Lighthorse, and I'm proud of it. *That's* what I learned once upon a time."

She tilted her chin and the light hit her cheekbones, turning her skin to gold. Dan caught his breath. She was so beautiful—so fascinating both inside and out—how could anyone have seen her as anything less than priceless? He wanted to find those people and tear them limb from limb. Perhaps he and Olaf had more in common than Dan had thought.

"I still don't understand why anyone would care what you looked like in college."

"This was over ten years ago. We had problems up here with treaty rights. Sovereign nation versus the state. Screaming matches in the night." At his blank look, Grace raised her eyebrows. "It was on the news every night."

"I wasn't here ten years ago. I was in Arizona." *Miserable,* his mind added. But he wasn't going back to Arizona, so there was no need to hyperventilate. Just reassuring himself of that made Dan's breathing slow into the normal range.

"Tensions were high back then. No one liked Indians."

"Is that why you didn't go home when you moved back to Wisconsin?"

"Mostly. Even though things have settled down a bit, the anger still bubbles beneath the surface. The fact that my father was on the legal team for the tribe did not endear him to the populace, no matter how hard he tried to walk the line between two worlds."

"You're angry at him still." Dan could hear it in her voice.

The look she gave him seared right to his belly. He'd hit the nail on the head, but she didn't like his insight much.

"Maybe. Nothing I did was ever right enough for him. Yet it was all right for him to be whatever *he* wished to be." She shrugged. "I worked for him while I went to massage school. He *loved* that."

Her sarcasm confused him. "Loved what? Your working for him?"

"That, he loved. He wanted me to be a doctor, or a lawyer—definitely not an Indian chief, or a massage therapist."

"You lost me."

"My grandparents are some of the few full blood Ojibwe left. They pitched a fit when my father married my mother. But he took one look at her and *bam.*" She smacked her palms together. "It was like lightning, he said. Love."

Dan couldn't help but smile. He liked stories, and Grace was a very good storyteller.

"Funny thing, my mother was the free spirit, my father the driven one. What he loved in her, annoyed the heck out of him in me. My grandparents came to adore my mother, because through her they were able to teach me all that my father had turned his back on."

"But he represented the Ojibwe, you said. He didn't turn his back on them."

"Not the tribe, or their treaty rights, true. But he wanted nothing to do with *being* Ojibwe. My grandparents still live in the same house where Dad was born. They prefer to live simply. My dad couldn't wait to get out."

"Not such an uncommon story."

Grace shrugged. "He wanted to be exactly what he was: a famous, respected attorney. He was on all the newscasts. He protected the treaty rights. And he died for it. The doctors told him to slow down. I told him. He was too busy making a name, and trying to get me to be his partner." Guilt colored her voice but she kept going. "My mother never recovered from his death. She lives on a lake in Minnesota. All alone with her pictures of him."

Dan had never had much of an imagination, but Grace conjured quite an image. If he closed his eyes he could see her mother, staring at the lake from the porch of a lonely cabin, holding tightly to a picture of the man she had loved and lost.

Dan blinked very fast and changed the subject. "You didn't want to be a lawyer?"

"Hell, no. I saw what it did to him. The hours, the pressure, the need to help everyone, all the time. I want to help people, but I want to help them live, not wage legal battles half the time they can't win. My dad didn't understand. He called me a touchy-feely flake, figured I'd give it up eventually and join him. I was too smart to keep at such nonsense all my life."

Nice way to talk to your kid, Dan thought, but he'd heard the same line often enough himself. "Just how smart are you?"

"Smart enough to know I'm no lawyer. No doctor, either. My father thought I was betraying everything he stood for, everything he'd fought for. He believed we needed to be more than we'd ever been before to take our people forward. I think everyone just needs to be who they are."

Her face had a sad cast that might have been a trick of the light, but the slump of her shoulders and the heaviness in her voice made Dan think the light did not trick him at all.

"I think you're right, and I like who you are."

"Oh, really?" She raised her eyebrows and leaned her elbows on the table. The sadness had fled, and she was confrontational once more. She made him dizzy for more reasons than one. "Then why are you trying to take away what's important to me? Project Hope is right, too. It's who I am. It's what those sick kids need."

For just a moment Dan wanted to agree. He wanted to give her everything she asked. But if he did that, everything *he'd* spent years working toward, all he'd given up, all he'd turned his back upon, would be worthless. His research would never come to fruition, and everything his parents had said would happen when he'd refused to be who they wanted him to be and insisted he had to be who he was, would happen. Grace, of all people, should understand that.

"I can't. You see I—"

"Em! Em! What's the matter, sister?"

A dull thump from the kitchen and a muffled cry sent the blood from Grace's face. She leapt to her feet and ran for the doorway. Dan was right behind her.

The scene that awaited Grace in the kitchen nearly sent her heart into failure. Em lay on the floor, pale and wan, her hand to her chest, eyes closed, breathing erratic. Ruby and Garnet fluttered around, each patting a shoulder—flustered, helpless, terrified.

Dan bumped into Grace, causing her to stumble a few feet into the room. At least that got her moving instead of standing there imagining the funeral. She couldn't function if she couldn't think, couldn't move.

"What happened?" Thankfully her voice came out brisk, with no hint of the panic that coursed through her veins. If she didn't keep a cool head, the Jewels would lose what little control they possessed. She'd seen that happen before, and it was not pretty.

"Em said her chest hurt, then she slid down on the floor." Ruby's voice shook.

Grace put the back of her hand to Em's forehead. Damp but not clammy. Still, she didn't care for those shallow, panting breaths.

"What should we do, Doctor?"

Ruby's question brought Grace's head up in surprise. She always handled health-related crises in this house. Though this looked to be the worst crisis yet.

Grace glanced over her shoulder to find Dan filling the entryway, looking trapped, despite the lack of a door to keep him contained.

"Uh, I'm not . . ." He looked at Grace helplessly.

"He's not that kind of doctor," Grace filled in.

"Pshaw! A doctor's a doctor. He went to school, didn't he?"

True enough, Grace thought. He had the training, even if he didn't choose to use it. She was scared enough by Em's color to say, "You could just look, couldn't you?"

"I think the first thing to do is call 911."

"There is no 911."

"What?" Panic lit Dan's voice. He really wasn't that kind of doctor—one who thrived on emergency, anyway. He looked nearly as pale as Em.

"There isn't a hospital for forty miles. This isn't New York City."

"What do you do in an emergency?"

"Drive very fast. Or if you can't drive, you call the hospital, and then you wait."

"People can die that way."

"All the time." Her voice broke.

A cool yet surprisingly strong hand clamped onto Grace's wrist. She looked into Em's pain-filled eyes. "No hospital, Grace. Just Dan."

Grace looked up at Dan and let him see everything she feared. "Please?" she whispered.

He closed his eyes, as if fighting both her plea and himself. For a moment she feared he would flee, and while she knew she could deal with the crisis if she had to, for some reason she wanted him with her.

When he opened his eyes the uncertainty had receded, and he strode into the room, then knelt next to Grace and Em. He pried Em's hand from Grace's wrist and checked the pulse, shrugged. "A bit fast, but not so bad. Where does it hurt?"

Em patted between her breasts. *Clunk, clunk.* Grace reached out and thumped her knuckle against Em's breastbone. Something hard lay beneath the gold and silver dress.

Dan looked like the snake on Em's headdress had leapt off and bit him. "What's that?"

"Corset, dear," Em whispered. "Couldn't get into the dress without one. I'm not the girl I used to be."

"Corset? A real corset—laces, whalebone, the whole nine yards?"

"What other kind is there?"

Dan cursed. "No wonder she passed out. We have to get her out of that thing. Corsets killed women in the old days all the time. I'm sure they still work just as well."

Grace started to hyperventilate. She couldn't lose Em. She wouldn't. She'd had the Jewels with her, in one combination or another, all her life. Now that her mother had lost her path and her father had traveled farther on his, Grace didn't know if she could bear losing Em, too.

With Grace on one side and Dan on the other, they helped Em sit up. Dan reached for the back of the dress, fumbled a bit, then stopped with his hands hovering, uncertain, above Em's neck "It's locked."

Grace searched for a button, a zipper, a key. Nothing. "You're right. Em, how did you get into this thing?"

Em just gasped and got whiter.

"Hooks and eyes," Ruby put in from the corner of the kitchen, where she and Garnet huddled, hand in hand. "All the way down."

Dan fumbled some more, but his too-big hands were unable to release the small fastenings.

"I feel light-headed again," Em murmured, and then she slumped into a faint. Ruby and Garnet cried out and hugged each other.

Grace shoved Dan's fingers aside and tried herself. She got one fastening open, but her hands shook so badly she couldn't even find the next one. So panicked was she at Em's plight, Grace barely noticed when Dan got up and went to the counter.

He returned, put his hands over hers, and stilled

them. "She's going to have a fit, but this isn't funny anymore," he said.

Grace had no idea what he meant until he grasped the sides of the dress and yanked it in half with a single outward motion of his powerful hands. Tiny hooks and eyes popped all over the place, pinging against Grace like needles of rain and scattering across the floor with a sound reminiscent of the same rain on a hot tin roof.

Dan picked up the filet knife, stuck the point beneath the corset strings, and with a single upward flick of his wrist, cut them loose. Immediately Em took a full, deep breath.

So did everyone else.

Ten

Dan's chest felt tight. He'd been really scared there for a minute. Em could have died if he'd been wrong. But she hadn't. Only Grace's trust and faith in him had kept Dan from panicking. This was why he was a doctor without patients. Pain and emotion made him want to help people so badly he forgot everything he knew. Sad, but true.

Gently he laid Em back on the floor. She opened her eyes and looked at him with adoration. "That feels so much better, Doctor, thank you."

Kneeling next to her, Dan felt like the tallest guy in town. When Grace put her hand over his where it rested upon his knee, her touch reached all the way to his wildly beating heart. "My hero," she whispered.

Dan felt like one. Maybe this doctor-patient thing wasn't so bad. Maybe he'd never given it a good look-see. He'd stuttered and shuffled and felt like a fool, then decided research was his forte—and it was. He was very, very good at going into the zone and coming out with the truth. But sometimes the zone got lonely. He'd never noticed how lonely until Grace came along.

"My chest still hurts," Em said.

Dan's heart did a swan dive into his belly. Maybe he wasn't such a doctor after all. "Where?"

She pointed to her diaphragm. "It burns, like after I eat too much pickled herring and jalepeños."

"Ahh!" Ruby and Garnet agreed and rubbed their bellies in exactly the same spot as Em.

Dan blinked. "You eat that?"

"Doesn't everyone?"

Dan shook his head. "Did you eat that today?"

"No. Only carrots, cauliflower, broccoli."

"Raw?" She nodded. "All you ate today were raw vegetables?"

"The bran muffins and oatmeal were cooked."

Dan moaned. "No wonder you're in pain. You ate too much roughage. Your stomach is working like a cement mixer trying to digest that. I think you'd better take it easy on the raw veggies. Maybe cook a few once in awhile?"

"That's all?" Grace asked, relief evident in her voice. "Indigestion?"

"I'd like her to go to a hospital, or at least her family doctor. Couldn't hurt."

"I don't have a family doctor, just you," Em said.

"I'm not—"

"That kind of doctor. I know. But you examined me, you gave your diagnosis, and I like it."

"I could be wrong. What if there's something serious I missed?"

"What if?" Em struggled to her feet.

"You could die."

"I could get hit by a truck, too, but I'm not planning on it."

Dan was starting to feel as if he were arguing with Olaf. Speaking of who. . . . He glanced uneasily at the door, expecting the big man to come busting in, take one look at Em's tattered dress and slug him.

When Olaf didn't appear at the most inopportune time for a change, Dan relaxed a tiny bit, then helped Em to her room, settling her on the bed.

"Thank you, Doctor, you saved my life."

"Not really," he said, though he couldn't help but smile.

"I choose to think so."

"And what you choose is true?"

"Life works out so much better that way."

"I just bet it does."

"You should try my way sometime. Choose to believe, and what you choose will be true."

"And if it isn't?"

Em frowned. "That's never happened."

"Never mind." Grace nudged Dan aside. "Lie down, Aunt Em, and I'll take care of everything." Grace sat on the end of the bed and untied, then removed, the Egyptian crisscross sandals. Grace lifted Em's feet into her lap and began to massage them.

"What are you doing?" Dan asked, feeling as if he were intruding on an intimate ritual.

"Reflexology. To make her pain go away."

"Never heard of it."

"I can't imagine you would have. There are points on the feet that correspond to points on the body. Right here . . ." She pushed on the pad of the left foot. "Is for the heart. And here . . ." She shifted her thumb to the arch and smoothed across the width of the foot, then swept upward. Em's lips compressed at the pressure. "Corresponds to the stomach."

"You believe that?"

"It works."

Dan's happy little bubble of joy burst. Everything was going just fine, then, out of the blue, Grace starts up some hip-hop New Age foot stuff. He'd never understand her.

"That works because Em believes it does. Like a placebo. A sugar pill."

Grace let out an exasperated sigh and turned to Dan. "So? If it works, it works. Go away."

Dismissed, just like that. So much for being her hero.

Dan went away.

Grace took out her annoyance on Em's feet. Reflexology required continuous pressure at specific points. Right foot for problems on the right side of the body, left foot for the left. Sometimes the treatment hurt a bit, especially when you hit the part of the foot related to the injury you wanted to heal. But if you could bear the treatment, the relief was worth the trouble.

The first time Grace had reflexology performed on her, she'd been bent nearly double with a pulled stomach muscle from her first aerobic dance class, which had been her last aerobic dance class. She'd been in pain for a week—slowly stooping over, inch by agonizing inch, to ease the pain. Nothing worked—cold compresses, hot packs, pain relief medicine, rest—nothing. She was at the end of her rope, then Olaf had done her feet. The next morning she was fine.

Placebo? Sugar pill? Faith? Whatever. If it worked, do it; that was her motto. Dr. Dan could just blow his opinion out his ear. She'd like to see what shade his face would turn if she tried Reike—the ancient art of healing with the hands.

"Are you better now?" Grace whispered, not wanting to wake her aunt if the woman had fallen asleep.

"Mmm-hmm."

"Pain gone?"

"Yes, dear. Bless you."

Grace smiled as the tender feeling she loved so much stole over her. When she made someone's pain go away the warm, fuzzy glow that filled her chest reminded her why she did what she did every day. And when she soothed the pain of a child, the feeling exploded like a firecracker at midnight.

" 'Night." Grace opened the door.

"Sleep tight," Em murmured. "Love you."

"Love you more."

Grace went to her office and sat at her cluttered desk. Why was she so annoyed with Dan?

Because tonight he'd seemed to fit right into her happy home as no other man ever had? Then he'd acted like a stiff again, right when her guard was down. When she thought she could trust him, he'd taken her beliefs, her career, and disparaged them with one sentence and a flicker in his eyes. How could he do that so easily? Because he was who he was, and she'd best not forget that.

How could the man be both adorable and abominable at the same time?

"Aren't they all?" she asked no one in particular, then gave a wry laugh. At least the ones you liked the most always turned out to be more on the abominable side than not.

She turned her chair and stared out at the night, though she did not see or enjoy the moon and the stars. No wishes tonight; her mind was occupied with less fanciful things. Grace had long ago put the painful part of her past behind her, and most times she refused to remember all that had happened. But now she took the memory out and probed that past like a sore tooth.

Once upon a time she'd felt the same riot of emotions she felt now for Dan Chadwick. Not quite as fast as she'd felt them for Dan, nor quite as strong. Then she'd called the feelings love. Now she knew a whole lot better.

Men like Dan did not take women like Grace seriously. Chambermaids remained chambermaids, though princes usually turned out to be frogs.

And forever after? Ha, ha, ha.

Em got disgusted with her attitude, because to Em, God had given her the world as a great big playground, and men were the best toys in it. But Grace was not Em, and she never would be.

Grace *had* believed in forever after once. She'd hoped, and she'd dreamed, and she'd truly thought she'd found the man to share her life with. Then she'd heard him describe her as "one of the natives." Good for a tumble but never a ring—at least not for an up-and-coming attorney with political aspirations, a son of the social elite.

Just remembering that night, his voice, her pain, made Grace's eyes water. She had loved Jared with all her stupid young heart, believing, since he was a colleague of her father's, that who and what she was okay with him.

And it had been, for an affair.

Was Jared the reason Dan pushed all her buttons? Dan looked nothing like Jared. Jared had been suave, tall, debonair, polished and slick. Dan was . . . well, Dan. Clumsy like a puppy and just as earnest, huge as Olaf, and brilliant as the sun on the water at noon.

Dan was a doctor—kind of. Jared had been a lawyer all the way. She was *not* falling for the same kind of man twice, no matter what Olaf muttered. She wasn't falling for Dan at all. This was business and she would remember that. No more kisses, no more touches, no more dinners, or even long lunches.

Thinking in verse. I must be tired.

She was, quite frankly, exhausted. But before she went to bed, she had to discover the truth about one thing that was driving her crazy.

Grace went to an overloaded shelf of books and dragged out a medical text from massage school. Most of her books had been about bones and muscles, but one had been about everything under the sun. Grace hefted the tome onto her desk very carefully. If she dropped this one on her foot she'd probably break a bone.

She turned to the index. "Paronychial infection, where are you?"

* * *

Dan was working when headlights swept up his driveway and glared into the front window. He had not made it into the zone yet, or he'd never have noticed them at all. He'd been too preoccupied with Grace and his feelings for her to think clearly about what to do with his bottles and beakers.

How could Mrs. Cabilla have thought Grace would help his research? He couldn't think straight for thinking of her. Though Mrs. Cabilla hadn't been around to see him mooning over Grace, she knew what Grace looked like. She knew how Grace was.

The door burst open—he'd forgotten to lock it again—but why way out here? Like a crazed thief would come and steal the cure to paronychial infection? Even if he had one.

Grace stood in the doorway and Dan frowned, wondering if he'd conjured her from his imagination. That would be a good trick since he'd never had much of an imagination—at least before he met Grace.

"Magi-manidoo!" she spat. *"Barba'risk! Bavia'n. Bete!"*

"English, Grace."

"You—you—you doctor! You stiff! You impossible, abominable—" Her mouth worked as if she was searching for a suitable epithet. "Very bad man."

"As cussing goes, you've got a lot to learn. But you've got the voice and the sneer just about right. You want to tell me what I did?"

Her gaze swept the room. Slowly, with the swaying walk that was all hers and usually turned Dan's mind to Jell-O, she approached. When he saw her hands clenching and unclenching, he heard again the sound of breaking glass from Olaf's room that morning, and he stepped between her and his work. He hadn't wanted to be on this side of Grace's temper, but it looked like he was. If he could only figure out what he'd done, he might be able to diffuse her.

She came so close the scent of cinnamon and spice wafted over him. His mind did the Jell-O jiggle. Then she stomped on his foot and the pain brought him back. Diffuse her? Maybe not.

"Paronychial infection is . . . is . . ." Her voice came through clenched teeth.

"Infection of the nail bed. What about it?"

"Aargh!" She threw up her hands and began to pace like a caged wolf. "You're trying to find a cure for ingrown toenails?"

"Not exactly."

"Close enough. That's what this"—she waved her hand at the laboratory behind him—"is all about?"

He shrugged, unable to understand what had made her so mad. "I thought you knew that."

"I knew you were trying to cure para, pora—some kind of infection. Something serious."

"It is serious. By discovering the cure to one infection, you can discover the cure to countless others."

"I thought you were dealing with life-and-death stuff. I felt *guilty!* How could you try and take my grant for toenail rot?"

Dan was getting mad now, though with Dan, anger rarely showed. He got more proper the higher his blood pressure rose—just like his father before him.

"I am *taking* nothing. The grant was mine long before you showed up."

"Showed up? I live here!"

"I don't think people in glass houses should throw stones, do you?"

Her eyes narrowed, and Dan really wished he had not mentioned anything about throwing stones and glass. He glanced at his work, but there was no way, even with his huge body, that he could protect it all.

When he looked back, Grace had stepped closer. "Classical quotes at this time of night? Spare me. Just explain what you're insinuating with your glass houses talk and your high-and-mighty attitude."

Perhaps he would do better to advance than to retreat. She was so focused on him, she'd forgotten his work. If she'd ever cared at all. Dan stepped away from the glass and went toe-to-toe with Grace.

"I'm not insinuating anything. I'm saying right out—you've got nerve trying to steal the grant from me so you can make blankies."

"That's it!" Grace shoved him. Caught off guard, he grabbed her elbows. When she bumped into his chest, he kissed her.

She made a sound deep in her throat, fury or passion, he wasn't sure which. A moment later, he didn't care. When his mouth touched hers, all coherent thought fled.

His hands flexed on her shoulders, learning the shape of the fine bones beneath her shirt, beneath her skin. Strength and fragility; the contrast aroused him. He cupped her face, tilted her mouth, stroked those cheekbones that shaped her beautiful eyes. His own eyes were closed, yet still he could see every

nuance of her face as if the image had been burned
into his brain.

When she didn't kick him in the shin, stomp on
his foot, or knee him in the—Dan shifted so he
could prevent that option, just in case—but started
to kiss him back, Dan forgot why he'd kissed her in
the first place, and just kissed her.

His tongue stroked her lips, and she opened them
for him on a sigh that sounded of his name and the
night. She tasted of honey, lemon, and something
else, dark and rich, as unidentifiable as the need
that rolled between them. Was it lust or something
more? What did it matter? It was.

In the back of his mind he knew he should not
be kissing her—not here, not now, not for whatever
reason he'd begun to in the first place. But as usual,
he had no control where Grace was concerned.
When she reached up and shoved her fingers
through his hair, holding his mouth on hers, strok-
ing his lips, tickling his tongue, tasting his teeth,
control became a memory he could not quite remember.

He wanted her in his arms more than he'd ever
wanted anything else, so he dropped his hands from
her face and wrapped them around her body. Her
fingers twined about his neck, and the front of her
pressed to the front of him. Once upon a time he
might have been embarrassed by the condition of
his body. But once upon a time he had not known
Grace.

She did not flinch; she did not shift away from
the obvious proof that he was glad to see her, but
she did stop kissing him. And while he wanted to

pull her back, and kiss her some more, when she put her hands on his chest and said, "Stop," he stopped.

When she said, "Let me go," he let go.

When she looked at him with big, confused eyes, he stared back with confused eyes of his own.

"You can't just kiss me every time I say something you don't like."

"I can't? It worked for me."

"I noticed."

Dan blushed. He'd been wrong to say Grace could not embarrass him. Grace could make him feel anything she wanted him to feel. That truth, combined with the lack of control he exhibited around her began to irritate him, as much as the reason for her visit.

"It didn't work for me," she continued. "You might make me forget who I am, what I want, what's important, for a moment. But when we stop kissing, the problem's still there."

"I seem to have forgotten tonight's problem."

"Let me refresh your memory. You're taking money to find a cure for something that doesn't need to be cured."

"Refresh my memory some more—you got your medical degree where?"

Those lips he liked so much when they were pressed to his own thinned into an angry line once more, and the confusion in her doe-brown eyes fled. "Why don't you use your own money for this nonsense?" she snapped.

"Nonsense? One man's nonsense is another

man's dream. I would think you of all people would understand that."

"What are you talking about?"

"You think my medical research is nonsense, well your blankie-drop is nonsense to me."

"You don't know anything about it. Just like all the rest—you look at me and you think I'm a flake. What I believe can't be anything but the ravings of a first-class space cadet. If it's important to me, well then it must be nonsense!"

Uh-oh, she could go from kiss Dan to kick ass in a matter of seconds. Dan's head spun at the change and he scrambled to keep up. "Now, Grace—"

"You don't *hear* anything, Dan! You don't listen. You're just like all those stiffs at all the hospitals. When I try to tell them what I'm doing, they just nod and walk away. And when I come back the next time, they don't remember I was there the first time at all. It's as if I don't exist."

"You exist, Grace."

"You know you've never once asked me what my project is about?"

He frowned. "Blankets for seriously ill children."

"But why, Dan? Did you ever ask me why?"

He shrugged. "Why?"

"Meet me at St. Mary's Hospital tomorrow at ten, and I'll try to explain it in a language you can understand, doctor boy."

She walked out without a backward glance, and when she slammed the door, one of the test tubes he'd been trying so hard to protect rolled off the table and shattered.

"Figures," he muttered to the suddenly silent room.

Grace growled in time with the stomp of her feet. "Men, men, men, men." From the driveway, to the front walk, up the porch steps, and into the house.

Olaf's boat was parked in the driveway, but the house was dark. The murmur of voices upstairs somewhere drifted to her. Either the Jewels were talking or a television was on.

Since she didn't want any of the Jewels getting out of bed at 3 A.M. to shut off their televisions—contraptions saved from the days before remote controls—then breaking a hip when they tripped on a slipper or a discarded headdress, she would shut off any wayward episodes of Jay Leno before she went to her own bed.

Grace climbed the first flight of stairs. Just being home calmed her. All the people who loved her, understood her, supported her, lived beneath this roof. As long as she was home, everything would be all right.

She'd been steamed all the way back here. Heck, she'd been steamed all the way to Dan's, and the temperature, both within her and without, had not cooled off any while she was with him. It never did. The man touched her and she melted. Embarrassing but true.

What *was* that?

Whatever it was, it had to stop. She'd be the flake he thought she was if she continued to wrap herself around his excellent body every time he so much as brushed it against her. She had to at least pretend to be a professional—even though pretending had never been her strong suit. Grace was who she was. Take her or leave her. Unfortunately, lately, most people chose the latter option.

Tomorrow she would show Dan what Project Hope was all about, and then it would be his turn, under Mrs. Cabilla's dictum, to help her. They'd see if he had better luck with the powers that be than she had.

The continued murmur of voices drew Grace toward Em's room. She'd planned to check on Em last, so she could stay and chat or work her aunt's feet one more time if necessary. But a glance at Ruby's, then Garnet's, doors revealed no lights, flickering or otherwise. The narrow glow from their night-lights revealed aunt-shaped lumps in the beds.

So who was in Em's room?

Grace crept down the hall. No shouts, no cries, no thumps—it could not be an intruder, could it?

Her heart beat out a cadence of fear. Should she call the police right away? No, best to get Olaf. He was better than any policeman, because he was right here, right now. But she had to pass by Em's room to get to the stairs that led to Olaf's attic abode. Slowly, she crept down the hall.

Just outside Em's door, the voices became clear, and Grace stopped creeping and started to eavesdrop. She couldn't help herself.

"Get out of my room, you big oaf."

"O-laf, not oaf. Has your illness jumbled your mind, my Em?"

"I'm not ill, and I'm not your Em. What I am is tired. Go away."

Grace frowned. It wasn't like Em to be so impatient. And especially with Olaf. Em had always treated him like a great big, overly cuddly, slightly annoying dog.

"You have scared me unto dying, Em. When I came to my home and discovered you ill my own heart fell about my ankles. If you would marry me and be my love we could have so many happy nights. I would not be out clog-dancing with other women, and you would not be wearing too-small clothes for other men."

Grace gaped as Em sighed. "I've told you before, Olaf, I'm too old for you. You need a woman who can give you a family. You're still a young man."

"We have a family. You are my heart. Your sisters I adore; Gracie is like my own. It does not take shared blood to make a family, it takes love. And I love you all."

"Grace is not your own. You deserve a child, and for that you need a different woman than me. Even thirty years ago, I couldn't have children."

"I had a child. She is lost. I do not wish to travel that road again. I wish to travel the rest of my life with you."

"You're being silly."

"No, you are. Love is a gift. You do not throw gifts to the ground and clog-dance all over them. You grab them with both your hands and hold them to your heart."

"I've had five husbands."

"And you are still here and they are all dead. What does that tell you?"

"I'm cursed?"

"No, you need a younger man for number six."

Grace smiled. Olaf had a point.

"I did so hate burying one after another. You promise I won't have to bury you?"

"Olaf promises."

"Ha, lying to me already. How can you promise that?"

"Because you do not *bury* a descendant of Vikings."

"Oh, really, what do you do with them?"

"I will tell you after."

"After?" Em giggled, and sheets rustled.

Grace fled. Though she might be happy that her partner and her aunt had found happiness, she did not want to wait around and listen to "before."

As she went back the way she'd come, she discovered Ruby and Garnet were not asleep after all. They stood smiling in the doorways to their rooms.

"Did sister and Olaf work things out?" Ruby whispered.

"Sounds like it."

"Hounds in the thicket?" Garnet said in a stage whisper. "I thought we were waiting for Em to kiss and make it with Olaf."

"They are!" Ruby snapped.

"Whose car?"

Grace took a step toward Garnet, meaning to explain at close range, but Ruby got there before her, shoved her sister back into her room and followed, shutting the door behind them. Frantic whispering followed before Grace heard, "Now if we can only get Grace to marry that nice young man, they can start having babies for us to play with."

"Uh-oh," Grace murmured. "Matchmakers at eleven o'clock."

No wonder Dan had been asked to dinner. She'd have to put a stop to any hopes in that direction. Sure, she and Dan were like a match and gasoline in the physical attraction department, but the very thought of them getting married was ludicrous. Their personalities were like oil and water. They'd kill each other before a year was out. No two people could be more different.

Leaving her aunts to continue their whispering beyond the closed door, Grace continued to her room. Flicking on the light, her gaze fell upon the picture of two laughing people, which she kept upon her nightstand.

The man was dark, handsome, intense, while the woman was blond, beautiful, ethereal. Her parents had been oil and water, too. Different as night and day, yet their marriage had been the stuff of dreams—until Joseph Lighthorse died. The empty ache in her mother's eyes had shown Grace she did not want to love a man so much that when you lost him you lost a part of yourself.

Just looking at the picture of her parents made Grace's eyes water. As she often did when things bothered her, and tonight she had a plate full of bothersome things, Grace picked up her crocheting. While her mind and hands were occupied with a repetitive task, her subconscious often picked at a problem.

She'd always felt like an outsider with her parents, an intruder even, on their perfect love. That was why having the Jewels around worked so well for everyone. Her aunts had doted on her as the child they'd never had. Grace had not lacked for attention, or for love.

Her family had always been considered odd—outcasts even before the treaty troubles. The fey Irish quiltmaker and the Ojibwe attorney made quite a pair. But what man wanted his wife's three sisters living with him?

Though Grace's father had denied living the Ojibwe way, he had been raised with the value of family. When he married his wife, he'd understood and accepted that her sisters would live with them, too. It also helped, when he worked day and night, for his wife to have her sisters to play with.

Grace finished the granny square, clipped the yarn and tied off the block. Shaking her head at the bitter cast to her memories, she tossed the block back into the bag next to her bed.

She'd had a happy childhood. Her parents had loved each other. Her mother had not complained about her father's career. She had understood what drove her husband, even if his daughter hadn't. Diamond Lighthorse may have become a hermit after losing the man she'd adored more than anything else, but while he'd been her husband, whatever he'd done had been fine with her—even working himself to death.

Grace wished she could say the same for herself.

Eleven

Dan arrived at the hospital promptly at ten, and Grace was nowhere to be found. Of course she'd only told him to be there; she hadn't told him exactly where.

So he stood around in the lobby feeling big and conspicuous and foolish, until he thought to ask at the desk for Grace Lighthorse. His real-world skills definitely needed brushing up.

"Certainly, she's here." The elderly clerk beamed. "Comes every week at least once, sometimes two or three times, and goes to the pediatric floor. Lovely girl—kind and giving. You know her?"

Dan nodded. "And the pediatric floor is . . . ?"

"Third floor. Elevator's down the hall on the right. Tell her I said hello."

Dan started down the hall. Everyone loved Grace, everywhere, it seemed. She must be the social butterfly of the century. So why was she having so much trouble getting Project Hope into hospitals?

Dan stepped onto the elevator and punched "3." Obviously everyone else thought the idea for Project Hope as silly as he did. So how was he going to live up to his part of the bargain they'd made with Mrs. Cabilla? Grace was living up to hers.

Bing! The elevator opened and Dan stepped out. Typical hospital floor: nurses' station, patient rooms, lounge. The only thing out of place was the laughter coming from one of the rooms on the other side of the hall.

Drawn despite himself, Dan walked toward the musical sound of a child's laughter and found Grace.

She knelt at the foot of the child's bed, her full, multicolored skirt swirled in a pool around her legs. The tip of one socked toe peeked out from beneath the hem, her shoes, no doubt, tossed into the far corner the moment she'd walked in the door.

A sock puppet covered each hand, and she ducked her head beneath the edge of the bed, waving those hands up high so the little girl, Becky Bouchamp, according to the door, could see the show.

"And *poof,* the genie disappeared," said the right hand, which looked like some kind of malformed dog.

"And everything was happy again," said the left hand, which looked not quite as good.

Becky giggled, drawing Dan's attention from the vision on the floor to the angel in the bed. Though her skin seemed unnaturally pale, her face was lit with joy. Huge, dark eyes sparkled in a tiny face, surrounded by very, very short brown hair. She looked like a pixie child in the midst of that big, white bed. In her hands she clutched the brightly colored cloth Grace had been sewing the morning Dan jogged to her house.

"Sometimes I'm still scared," said the right hand.

"Me, too," said the left hand.

"But at least we have each other." They hugged. "And even when we're all alone, we always have something to hold on to."

The right hand held up a square of peach flannel and scrunched the material in its fist—or rather, to its chest. Left hand did the same with a slice of green corduroy.

"Magic blankets!"

The two hands clasped in another hug, pressing the mini blankets between them. The little girl clapped and Grace sat up, putting her chin on the edge of the bed and grinning. Becky waved and laughed—a great, big belly laugh that seemed to overtake her entire body with glee.

Dan had very little experience with children. He saw them on the streets sometimes, and if they were well behaved they seemed pleasant enough. But this one was as cute as a kitten. That laugh kind of wrapped around a person's heart and squeezed. He wanted to hear her laugh again, so he held very still.

"So I'll come back and see you at the end of the week?" Grace stood. "By then I bet you'll feel a whole lot better."

The animation drained from the child's face like water from a sieve. "The doctors hurt me. But I don't get any better. Mommy cries. Daddy, too, when no one's looking."

Dan's heart squeezed with sadness this time, and he swallowed a sudden lump in his own throat. Another reason he'd decided to be a doctor without patients. Sometimes things went well and everything was okay and then other times . . .

"I'm sorry to hear that." Grace sat on the bed. "But now that you have the magic blanket, you'll never be alone."

Magic blanket? Dan frowned. He might not be a doctor with patients, but he knew better than that. Having the puppets believe in magic was one thing, encouraging such a belief in a sick child was another. Before Dan could say anything, Becky spoke, and the hope in her voice made him stay right where he was, with his mouth shut.

"I can sleep with it?"

"Sure."

"I don't sleep good here. It's too dark, and it's never really quiet."

"I know. That's rough. But sleep will help you feel better."

"Can I take my blanket when I go for tests?"

"If the nurses say it's all right, and I bet for most tests it will be."

Becky brightened even further. Grace leaned over and kissed the little girl on the forehead. As she straightened, Becky threw her arms around Grace's neck and held on tight.

Grace gathered the child onto her lap. For a long while they rocked—Grace, the little girl, and her new blanket. The scene was so peaceful, Dan didn't want it to end. But of course it did.

He leaned against the door in an effort to see better and the hinges creaked. Both Grace and the child glanced up and saw him. Their expressions, which had been soft, and warm, and full of joy, became guarded once more, and Dan wanted to kick himself for destroying the beautiful picture.

"Dr. Chadwick, how nice to see you." The ice in Grace's voice revealed the lie to her words.

"Doctor?" The panic in the child's voice made Dan hesitate before stepping into the room. She seemed to shrink in upon herself as he approached. Grace held her more tightly, and Becky inched the blanket up her face until only her eyes could be seen above the hem.

"I don't know you. Are you a new doctor? You aren't going to hurt me, are you?"

Dan froze in the middle of the room, uncertain what to say, unwilling to come closer and scare her any more.

"No, sweetie," Grace intervened, and her voice was no longer cold but warm as a summer day. "Dr. Chadwick's not that kind of doctor."

A surprised snort of laughter escaped Dan at hearing his own words turned around to the good for a change. The child, uncertain what was so funny, nevertheless, smiled at him, and he felt, for just a minute, how he'd felt when he'd kind of saved Em's life. Grace looked at him over the child's head, and when she smiled, too, his heart warmed.

For the first time he was glad to be "not that kind of doctor." For the first time he was glad to be exactly who he was—because Grace had smiled at him.

Grace kissed the top of the child's head and set her back on the bed. "I'll be back, Becky. You hold on to your magic blanket, and everything will look brighter. I promise."

Dan's joy evaporated. He'd forgotten about the magic blanket stuff. That really had to stop. "Grace—"

She held up a hand. "Be right there."

"I really don't think you should—"

The smile she'd given the child turned to a glare for him. "Take your opinion outside, Doctor. It wasn't asked for in here."

Dan hesitated, but a glance at Becky, who looked back and forth between the two of them with confusion in her eyes, made him move toward the door. "Bye, Becky, nice to meet you."

She waved and smiled sweetly, still clutching the magic blanket. Darned if she wasn't the cutest thing he'd seen in half a lifetime. Dan waited outside, feeling like a child sent to his room for insubordination at the dinner table.

A minute later Grace stepped into the hall and shut the door behind her. "For some reason, she likes you."

"Me?"

"That's what I said. Becky thinks you're cute."

"I thought I scared her."

"Once she knew you weren't that kind of doctor, you were just like the rest of the world—fit for Becky's love."

"Well, I've never been described as cute before."

"And probably won't be again."

"Hey!"

Grace looked him up, then down, in a slow perusal that made him hot all over in an instant. "One thing you are not is cute."

"What am I then?"

"A pain in the behind."

Her words hurt a bit, but he kept the hurt tamped down with all the others. Big, bruiser research scientists weren't supposed to be sensitive. "What did I do now?"

"I saw your face in Becky's room. You were going to say something about the magic blanket, weren't you?"

"Well, Grace, you have to admit—"

"No, I don't."

"Would you let me finish?"

"Do I have a choice?"

"What's that supposed to mean?"

"You'll give me your opinion regardless of if you know diddly about the subject."

"It's just common sense—"

"No, it isn't."

"But you have to admit—"

"I do not."

"Grace!" Dan said, a bit too loudly.

All the nurses at the desk and several in the hall turned to them and frowned.

"Shh," Grace hissed, and took his arm. "Let's take this to the cafeteria. You could use some tea."

"Tea?" Dan resisted the urge to stick out his tongue and make a gagging noise. The way Grace was dragging him off the pediatric wing, she'd probably ground him for life for inappropriate behavior.

As she hustled him toward the elevators, he did notice one thing. Every child who held a blanket cuddled it close.

Minutes later, ensconced in a corner table of the nearly empty cafeteria, Dan nursed a bottle of apple juice. Grace dabbed her herbal tea bag in the steaming water and stared at the swirling cinnamon surface.

He waited for her to speak, and when she didn't, he had to. "You told me you'd explain Project Hope in a language I could understand. I still don't understand."

Her gaze seemed far away, as if she were trying to figure out how to talk his language. Hell, half the time he didn't know.

"You saw Becky."

"What's wrong with her?"

"You know."

Dan nodded. He did. The pale, thin face; the short, short hair. "Will she . . . ?" He couldn't finish the sentence.

"No one knows. It's hope and pray time."

"How long have you known her?"

"An hour."

"No way."

Grace frowned. "What do you mean, 'no way?' "

"She was hugging you like you were her long lost best friend."

"She's a kid. I paid attention to her and gave her a present. Bingo, I'm her new best friend."

"Seriously?"

Her frown became an indulgent smile. "Seriously. The nurse called yesterday and asked me to bring Becky a blanket. She still has some tests and treatment to go through."

"The nurse called?"

Grace nodded. "The nurses support Project

Hope. They see how much the blankets help the kids."

"So why do you need the administration's approval if the nurses are calling you?"

"An isolated case here and there isn't enough. In order to give every child the opportunity to get what they need, the project must be approved at the top levels."

"What do the doctors think?"

"They think I'm a flake. Like you."

"I don't think you're a flake, Grace."

"No? But you were going to take me to task over my magic blankets, weren't you?"

"I don't think it's appropriate."

"Well, I don't think it's appropriate for a four-year-old to have cancer!" Her voice was a bit too loud and a bit too shrill. Grace's passion for everyone and everything only made her all the more fascinating to Dan. He'd never known someone who cared so much about so many.

She took a deep breath, swallowed some tea, and continued—more quietly, but no less intensely. "Sometimes all you can do is give them something to hold on to. But at least it's something."

"But telling them there's magic? Isn't that false hope?"

"Hope is never false—that's why it's called hope. If you believe in magic, magic happens."

"Bull."

Grace blinked a few times. "Well, don't spare my feelings, Dan. Tell me what you really think."

He ignored her sarcasm. "I still don't understand why you'd think this project warrants a grant from the Cabilla Foundation. This is charity work. Like doling out juice at a blood drive."

"Project Hope is no more a charity than your work is."

Dan flinched at the word *charity*. Grace reached down and yanked her huge purse into her lap. Dan figured she was pulling out the puppets, so she could explain in a language he'd understand. Instead, she extracted a three-ring binder and slapped it onto the table in front of him.

"Here." She opened the binder, stabbed her finger at the first page. "A language you can understand."

Dan leaned over and read the bold print. *Stress reduces immunity. Reduction of stress aids in fighting immune-deficient disease.*

He glanced at Grace. "True enough."

"Read on, Macduff."

Because children suspend their disbelief more easily than adults, who have learned to disbelieve, they are perfect candidates for trials. Preliminary studies in children have found that a sense of well-being aids in recovery. The more a child believes they will heal, the higher their chances of healing.

Dan continued to read and found himself caught up in the report. The research wasn't scientific, but it was intriguing, citing several cases where a child's diagnosis had turned around once their attitude improved, and one case where a terminal child had been cured completely.

"Placebo effect," he murmured.

"Pardon me?"

Dan looked at Grace. He'd been in the zone. Interesting. He glanced down at the binder. He'd read through the entire report. "Uh, I said placebo effect. They believe the blankets are magic, and so they are."

"And this is bad because . . . ?"

"It's not true."

"It isn't?"

"Come on, Grace, you don't believe in magic."

"I don't? What other word do you have for this?" She tapped the binder with her fingernail.

"Placebo."

"Magic. Placebo. You're splitting hairs, doctor boy. Hope. Faith. Believe in the power of what you can't see."

"You don't actually think your blankets can cure children, do you?"

"So what if they don't?"

Dan gaped. He probably looked like a fish out of water, gasping for air on the banks of Lake Superior. This entire conversation made his head ache. "So what? You give a child a blanket. You tell them it's magic, and it doesn't work. They die! That's terrible."

"I give them a blanket. I tell them it's magic. They have something to hold on to, and they feel safer, stronger, happier. That's magic. So sue me."

Dan's entire house of cards began to crumble before his eyes. What did science mean if all you had to do was believe in magic, and magic happened? Dan still didn't quite buy that, but the research in his hands was so intriguing, he felt the pull of the zone right here in the middle of town.

"This child." He flipped to the case that intrigued

him the most. "The one in the last stage who went into remission."

"Hope."

Dan frowned. "Yes, we've been over that."

"No, her name is Hope. She's a miracle. The doctors are stumped." She smirked. "I love it when that happens."

"She's fine?"

"Completely. Lives in Minneapolis. She's in high school now. Still sleeps with her blankie." Grace reached into her bag and pulled out the scrap of peach flannel the right-hand puppet had cuddled. "She gave me a swatch for luck. I'd say it's pretty lucky, wouldn't you?"

"And you named your project after her?"

"Why not? I told her I wouldn't stop. That I'd keep helping kids. I don't make promises I can't keep. I saw that child. She was almost an angel. She believed, and she survived. I believe. Admit it, Dan, don't you want to believe, too?"

Dan looked into her eyes and saw the Pied Piper. He did want to believe. He wanted to throw years of research to the wind and start studying her project. But if he gave up on paronychial infection when he was so close he could taste it, he'd never respect himself in the morning—and his parents would never respect him at all.

Dan straightened and shut the binder. "I'm supposed to be helping you with 'the stiffs,' as you so elegantly put it. Which stiffs have you spoken with, and what have you said?"

She was silent for a moment, perhaps sensing his withdrawal, then she sighed and tugged the binder back to her side of the table. "I've spoken with the administrator of St. Mary's and the chief of staff. I also tried several hospitals in Minneapolis before we moved here. Everyone thought my idea was a great big joke."

"Please tell me you didn't tell them you had magic blankets for the children."

"All right, I won't tell you."

Dan groaned. "Jeez, Grace. What did you wear? What did you say?"

"I wore my favorite bone through my nose and rings on my toes. I said, 'Ugga-wugga, smelly cheese, won't you approve my project, please?' "

"Grace, be serious. If this is how you talk to the administrators and doctors around here, no wonder they won't take you seriously."

"What does how I dress have to do with anything?"

"Nothing. I agree. But sometimes you have to play their game to get them to play yours."

"I don't play games."

"You'd better start. These guys like to say no; that's why they have the jobs they have."

"So what do you suggest?"

"Did you show them that?" He indicated the binder.

"If I could have gotten past, 'Hello, I'm Grace Lighthorse,' I would have."

Dan ground his teeth. He could see the scene in his mind. Grace so earnest, so hopeful, so bright and shiny, she made your eyes hurt. And the stiffs, as he was beginning to think of them, too—looking down their noses, elbowing each other, and laughing

behind her back when she left. Just the thought
made him want to do violence. But since Dan was
not a violent man, he would handle things the way
his father would.

By talking them to death.

He picked up Grace's binder. "Can I borrow
this?"

"What for?"

"I'd like to look at it awhile."

She shrugged. "Feel free."

He didn't think he knew how, but he was starting
to wonder if he might like to. Dan shook his head
to clear it of the images that seemed to invade his
habitually preoccupied brain all too frequently of
late. Grace made him think of silly things—moonlight on water, sunshine turned to rain, purple di-
nosaurs dancing through acres upon acres of
evergreen trees and little girls who were almost an-
gels but smelled like fresh oranges and cinnamon
toast.

Dan stood and his chair scraped back. "I'll see
you at the lab."

He didn't wait for her to question his abrupt
departure or even say good-bye before he fled the
cafeteria. Only a few minutes later he was ushered
into the offices of Dr. Randal Moss, head cook and
bottle-washer at St. Mary's Hospital. In other words,
the main administrative honcho, a man of Dan's
father's circle.

"Daniel!" Moss came around the desk with a
hearty smile on his face and pumped Dan's hand
like it was the air compressor on a beer keg.

Dan's lips twitched at the comparison. Dr. Moss

wouldn't know a keg from a cashew. He probably hadn't had a beer since high school, if then.

"Sir." Dan tightened his mouth to keep from laughing. What was the matter with him? Too much Grace, that's what. But he was here *for* Grace, so he'd better shape up.

"I was hoping you'd stop by and say hello. Your father told me the last time we spoke that you were doing a bit of work in my neck of the woods."

"Yes, sir. But I came here to discuss another project with you. Project Hope."

Moss's face still held a pleasant smile but his eyes went blank. He had no idea what Dan was talking about. And here Grace was hoping against hope that if she had got funding this man would let her do some good.

"Grace Lighthorse spoke to you recently. Security blankets for seriously ill children?"

"Ah, the Indian girl."

Dan's eye started to twitch. "I have her research here." Dan held up the binder. "It's quite good."

"You think so?" Dr. Moss made no move to take the binder, and Dan's hand fell. "Tell me again what it is you research, Daniel?"

Here we go, Dan thought. *Off come the gloves.* Moss might have met with him because of his father, but because Moss was like his father, he would also think that Dan was little short of a moron, despite his intelligence, to be doing what he was doing. That was why Dan preferred to do just about everything alone. Time to start talking the language of his father.

"My research is apart from the research of Miss Lighthorse. One has nothing to do with the other."

Moss ignored him. "Wasn't it toes?"

"Paronychial infection."

"Ah, yes. I'm supposed to take the word of a man who spends years trying to cure toenail rot?"

"Not rot exactly."

Moss shrugged. He could care less about anything but his own little world. As Dan had told Grace, men like Moss loved to say no. And Dan heard a great big no coming. Why had he thought he could out-talk a master like Moss? Just because Dan had been raised to be a stiff, and was one still according to Grace, didn't mean he was accepted by them. Or that he ever had been.

"Never mind." Dan tucked Grace's binder beneath his arm and prepared to go.

Unfortunately, Moss felt the need to get a few licks in for the enemy first. "You're an embarrassment to your parents. I don't plan to let you embarrass me with another of your hare-brained ideas."

"It's not my idea, it's Grace's. And it's a good one."

"Grace, huh? Well, that explains it. Don't get yourself in trouble, son. Or rather, get her in trouble."

Dan's eye was twitching so hard tears gathered at one corner and threatened to run down his face. He blinked rapidly, which only made the twitching worse.

"You okay?"

"Fine," he ground out. How did Grace keep going forward when all these stiffs were so backward?

"What would it take for you to give Miss Lighthorse's project a chance?"

"I can't think of a single thing."

"What if she got the Cabilla Grant?"

The barely contained amusement on Moss's face fled. "She's up for the Cabilla Grant? That's different. Mrs. Cabilla is well respected."

"Or at least her money is."

"Money makes the world go around. If the Indian girl's project gets funding like that, I'll give her research a look-see. But not before."

Dan sighed. Grace had been right. She needed the Cabilla Grant to gain respect in a world that should be above such things but sadly wasn't.

After thanking Dr. Moss, and agreeing to say hello to his father next time he spoke with him—sometime in the next millennium, maybe—Dan escaped the office, then the hospital.

Once outside he took a deep breath of warm, fresh air. He'd forgotten how playing the game, walking the walk, talking the talk of the establishment made him feel. Lightly soiled. He might not be a free spirit, but he wasn't one of *them* either.

He was right back where he'd started: Grace needed the grant; he needed the grant. If he got it, her project was doomed. If she got it, years of very important research would be no better than toenail rot. What were they going to do?

Dan looked at the binder he still clutched in his hand and got a very interesting idea. Grace's research was good, but he could make it better.

He looked up at the hospital with a considering

glance. He might not be like them, or want to be, but he knew what made them what they were.

Money talked, did it? So did prestige. Intelligence. Class.

But Dan knew what talked even louder.

Talk. Buzz. Gossip.

The medical profession was no different from any other. If he improved upon Grace's research, then let the cat out of the bag—accidentally on purpose—the resulting chatter would have hospitals lining up in droves, with or without the Cabilla Grant. The buzz would create opportunities for alternative funding. Dan could keep the Cabilla Grant. Grace's project would move forward. He'd find the cure he'd been searching for and the kiddies would get their blankies.

Grace arrived home to a coven of Jewels and one Norwegian masseur lounging in the quilt room. The four had their heads together, as they did every day, except Olaf's and Em's heads were attached—at the lips—which stopped Grace in mid-stride. Even though she'd overheard them last night, seeing them this morning still shocked her.

She was thrilled for them, but they should really get a room, she thought. Glancing at Ruby and Garnet, she found rapturous gazes upon their faces. They were thrilled for Em, too. Looked like husband number six would take his place in the family Bible real soon—if there was any room left for his name.

Ruby saw her in the doorway. "Grace, you're home."

Everyone looked up. Grace smiled, her gaze on Em. For a moment, Em looked nonplussed, after all she didn't know that Grace knew that . . . Well, whatever. Then Olaf stood and drew Em up to stand at his side.

"Gracie, my angel, your Aunt Em has consented to be my wife. I have loved her from the moment my eyes fell upon her. How could I not?"

Em punched his massive arm. "Maybe because I'm old enough to be your mother?"

"You are not! I am ever so much older than I look. Stop trying to talk me out of this, Emerald. What Olaf wants, Olaf gets."

"Uh, how old are you anyway?" Grace found herself asking. She'd never dared before.

"Old enough to know better than to tell, so do not ask me again. My life is complete and I will have no more arguments. Now, I have an appointment." He waved his hand at them. "Plan the wedding. Em will move in with me tonight. Once we marry, to an apartment we will go."

"Apartment?" The thought of Em leaving the house panicked Grace for a moment. Husband number five had died six years ago. Grace was kind of used to having Em around to talk to whenever the need arose. "Isn't this all kind of sudden?"

Olaf stopped in the doorway. "It is not sudden for me. It has taken forever. We are not children to be uncertain of our minds. We will not waste a minute now that Em has come to her senses." He strode off.

Grace turned to Em, who patted her on the arm.

"The town is small, honey. Wherever we move, it'll be like we're right next door."

Ruby and Garnet joined them, each patting Grace on a shoulder. "And we'll still be right here with you," Garnet assured her.

"You know we'd never leave you," Ruby added. "We'll start packing your things, Em."

The two moved out of the room, leaving Grace and Em alone. The sound of their bickering drifted from the hall as they made their way up to the third floor.

"I'll wrap the glass."

"A map of the grass? If you want to dig, you need to call the diggers hotline."

"Not a map. Wrap! Wrap! Never mind."

"They're going to drive you crazy, aren't they?" Em stared at her with a concerned frown.

"Why should today be any different than yesterday?"

Em didn't laugh; instead, she looked uncertain, which for Em was unheard of. "I guess they could live with us."

"I'm kidding," Grace assured her. "I've lived with those two all my life. I just tune them out, like you do. But if they left I'd miss them. Just like I'll miss you."

"We could all live in the house." She tilted her head. "But Olaf said newlyweds need some space."

"Of course you do. I'm being silly. It's just that everything is changing so fast."

"It is?" Em's gaze went from uncertain to shrewd in an instant. "Besides me marrying Mr. Muscles and getting our own place, what's changed?"

Grace shrugged. Em continued to stare at her, waiting. She always did that until Grace folded and told her everything. "I don't know." Throwing up her hands, Grace walked to the windows. "I feel squirrely all the time. As if I'm on the verge of something I can't see but should be able to."

"Let me guess, this started right about the time Dr. Magnificent showed up?"

Refusing to turn and meet her aunt's eyes—sometimes Em saw too much—Grace stared down at the hustle and bustle of Lake Illusion at lunchtime. "So what if it did?"

"You like him. He likes you. Why are you fighting this?"

"He's not for me, auntie. He'll hurt me in the end."

"You're clairvoyant now? When did that happen?"

Grace turned to face her aunt. "It doesn't take a clairvoyant to see what kind of guy he is. Olaf doesn't like him either."

"Olaf doesn't like anyone, except us, and you know it. That's Olaf. He sees you as his daughter." Em puffed up her chest and lowered her voice to imitate her brand-new fiancé. "And for a daughter of Olaf, no one is good enough." She let the air out of her lungs on a giggle. "He'd dislike the Dalai Lama. No one who wears a bedsheet could go near his Gracie. The fact that he hasn't tossed the good doctor into the lake ought to tell you something."

True enough. Still . . .

"Spill it, Grace. What is it about Dan that's got you all squirrely?"

Grace hesitated for another long moment, not

wanting to say aloud what was in her mind and bring all the pain of the past back to life. But maybe if she did speak of it, the past would lose its power to hurt her.

"He's just like Jared," she blurted.

"*How* is he just like Jared? He's got a wife stashed somewhere and a few kiddies to boot?"

Grace winced at that memory. Her perfect little dream world had burst when Jared walked into her father's funeral with the pristine wifey-wife, and the perfect son and daughter he had neglected to mention while whispering sweet nothings into Grace's ear.

Grief-stricken by her father's death, the betrayal of the second man she'd ever loved had been nearly too much. Hearing him joke at the burial about the benefits of slumming with the natives had pushed her over the edge.

The very next week, she'd moved, with her aunts and mother, to Minneapolis, and Jared had gone home to Washington where he'd belonged. She had not allowed a man close enough to touch since.

She'd never told anyone what she'd overheard, and she never planned to. Hearing someone she'd trusted with all of herself speak of her as if she were dirt had been worse than the sneers in her hometown, the whispers at college, and the veiled insults from the stiffs at the hospital. For the first time in her life she'd been embarrassed about who she was.

Over the grave of the father, who had spent a lifetime striving to be someone different than who he was, Grace vowed to always be herself and never be embarrassed again.

"Hey, earth to Grace?" Em waved her hand in front of Grace's face, effectively snapping her out of a past she did not care to remember.

"Uh, yes. I mean no. I don't think he has a wife." Grace sighed and her shoulders sagged. "But then I didn't think Jared had one either."

"Jared was a scum-sucking leach."

"True."

"If your father had been alive, or Olaf had been around, Jared would have been a very sorry slime-bucket."

"Also true. But Jared is past. I learned my lesson. I won't make the same mistake twice."

"I don't understand why you think Dan is like Jared." Em lifted one shoulder. "But you're the one who feels things about people. Did you ever stop to think why you're attracted to the same type of man?"

"I'm not following you."

"You say Jared and Dan are alike. And Jared and your father were alike, too."

Grace frowned. She didn't like where this was headed. "So?"

"Maybe you need a man like that."

"To drive me crazy all of my days?"

Em laughed. "You never know. Look at your mom and dad—they were two halves of one soul."

"And without Dad, Mom is half a person."

"I didn't want to mention this, but Diamond was always a wuss."

"Excuse me?" Grace had never heard her aunt speak ill of her mother.

"I lost five husbands, and I'm still functional. You gotta have some guts in life or get out."

"I'm probably more like Mom than you, Aunt Em. I just don't want to go there."

"But, sweetie, there is the best place on earth. You'll never be truly alive, truly happy, until you love with all your heart and give all of your soul."

"Loving Dan would be a big mistake."

"Mistakes?" Em shrugged. "I've made a few."

"Number four," Grace muttered.

"Number one wasn't my best moment, either. So what do you feel about Dan?"

"Green. He's green. Steady and sure."

"What's the matter with that?"

"He's also a stiff. Just like Jared. Just like the people at the hospital who won't give me a chance. Dan thinks I'm a flake."

"Does he really?"

"Yes."

"I think you're doing to him what you think he's doing to you." Grace cast a quick glance at her aunt, wondering if lusting after Dan's body showed plainly on her face. Em continued. "You're judging him on the surface. What he is to most people—doctor, research scientist, stiff, as you say—might not be *who* he is. You of all people should know better."

Em let that sink in for a moment before she continued. "I'm not any better. I looked at Olaf and saw a young man, a flirt—"

Grace choked. "Flirt? Olaf? Are you serious?" In her wildest imaginings, Grace could not imagine that.

"You've been in your own little world for a long time now, Grace. Who Olaf is on the surface is not who Olaf is deep inside. Inside, with me anyway, he is a great big flirt. Cute as a button."

"Olaf. Big guy? Hisses a lot? Shouts in Norwegian?"

Em nodded with an amused smile on her face. "Anyway, I couldn't see past the age difference, but Olaf isn't so narrow. He looked at me and saw 'desirable woman who isn't dead yet.' He saw what was inside, the adorable man, and I'll love him forever for that."

"I think what's on the outside of Dan goes all the way through to the inside."

"And would that be so bad? You're afraid he'll die on you like your dad? Or that he'll betray you like Jared?"

"Maybe both."

"Take a chance. Live a little. Just because Dan's different doesn't mean he's bad. Just different."

"I know."

"Do you? You've been trying so hard to be different from everyone else, to prove that different is okay, that different is somehow better, sometimes I wonder if you understand that being not so different is okay, too."

Hmm, Grace needed to think about that. *Was* she trying so hard to be different that she denied her true self? If that was true, then did she know her true self at all?

"And as for Dan, perhaps you need to look a little deeper inside that boy."

"See what isn't visible?"

"Find the man waiting to get out. Discover the person he can be with you—the man he can become—and the woman you could become with him."

Twelve

Two weeks of working with Grace in the morning and seeing Grace in his dreams all night—Dan was losing his mind. He was no nearer to finding his cure, and the zone escaped him, unless erotic daydreams counted as a type of zone.

At night, when he couldn't sleep because all he could think of was her, he cruised the Internet, faxed obscure research facilities like his own, and put together a much better binder for Grace's research than she had ever dreamed of having. Then he made phone calls and faxed more faxes.

If there was one thing Dan Chadwick knew, it was how to research something. He could prove any theory if given enough time. Except for his theory on paronychial infection. But he didn't want to think about that right now.

Because right now Grace was late—again.

He stared out the window at the lane that led to his house. No car, no Grace, no nothing.

She'd been acting kind of strange since that day at the hospital. Whenever he turned to stare at her, he'd catch her staring at him. Instead of yanking her gaze away, as most people would, she'd continue to stare at him as if off in a zone of her own.

She kept her distance, too. No more accidental touches, no more passionate kisses. Grace behaved as if she were deep in thought all the time, trying to figure out the mysteries of the universe, or maybe just a mystery closer to home.

She'd told him Em and Olaf were getting married, a bit of information that had floored Dan, as it seemed to have floored Grace. He could only hope that obtaining the woman of his dreams would make Olaf a bit less likely to kick Dan's behind into the next century, though somehow Dan doubted that.

He glanced at his watch again. Late, late, late. He was getting worried.

Dan put his forehead against the cool glass. Actually, Grace was never *really* late, but she was never on time, either. Five minutes, ten minutes, today fifteen. Each day she had a different excuse—excuses he didn't quite see as adequate, but she seemed to think they were.

The first day she said, "Baby ducks waddled across the road right in front of my car."

The second, "The cornfield had tassels, and the wind made them dance."

The third and the most confusing of all: "There were a thousand blackbirds in a freshly cut field. When they flew off, the sound of their wings filled the air and their silhouettes nearly blanketed the sun."

He had no idea why these things explained her being late. He should no doubt lighten up, but punctuality was part of his life. If he left an experiment unattended for too long, even if the blackbirds were flying, he could ruin weeks of work. So Dan always made sure he set his bells and whistles, just in case he went into the zone and forgot the time. That hadn't been a problem lately.

The crunch of tires on gravel announced Grace's arrival—sixteen minutes late. Dan stepped back from the window and waited for her to come in. The fact that he was actually looking forward to today's excuse, as if waiting for the news flash of the decade, annoyed him. They had work to do, and, sadly, no time to smell the roses.

"Morning." Her smile lit up his life. Unfortunately, this morning, he wasn't in the mood for lighting up. And anyway, Grace went right to the computer. Once in the lab she never dawdled. She worked—plain and simple. If she wasn't time-challenged, as well as such an incredible distraction to his libido, she'd be the perfect research assistant—intelligent, efficient, and quiet. Problem was, with Grace in the room his brain became mush.

"You're late," he said, surprising himself.

"I stopped to watch some kids going fishing." She flicked on the computer. A soft, sweet smile of remembrance lit her face, bright enough to rival the artificial light from the screen. "They looked like something out of a Norman Rockwell painting. Two boys, brothers I bet, with cane poles and a jar of worms, walking down the road. I watched until they turned off on a lane leading to one of the ponds. They were the cutest things I'd seen in a long, long time."

"You like kids."

She shrugged. "What's not to like? The aura of a child is the purest sensation on earth. White—with hints of every color in the spectrum."

Dan didn't know what to say to that. He didn't want to think about auras—children's or otherwise—he wanted to think about work. But because of Grace, he'd begun to notice all the things he'd been missing, and that was starting to annoy him.

"I wish you'd try to be punctual," he said, and even to him his voice sounded stuffy. Very like his father's. He hoped to God that invoking his father's name, and his father's style, while dealing with the hospital bigwigs had not caused an invasion of the body snatchers.

"I always try." Grace didn't seem very concerned.

"Can you try harder?"

She didn't even look at him, continuing to shuffle through papers. "What the heck? Sure. I can always try harder."

Dan sighed. "Grace, time that's lost can never be replaced."

She fixed him with an unreadable look. "My point exactly." Then she turned around and went to work without another word.

She'd agreed with everything he'd said, yet Dan felt as if they'd been talking about two different things, and he'd come out losing the round. He had no doubt she'd still arrive five minutes late tomorrow, and if he bothered to mention the lapse, she'd agree with him, and they'd start all over again. His head spun as it so often did when he was around Grace, for so many different reasons.

He had a week or less before Mrs. Cabilla, or

Perry, her weasel-faced minion, showed up. Then what was he going to do; what was he going to say? If he didn't have something more to show his bene-factress, Grace would win the grant. And though Grace's project intrigued him, the thought of five wasted years terrified him.

Dan truly believed in what he was doing or he wouldn't be doing it. And there was the tiny prob-lem of proving to his parents that he wasn't the fail-ure they'd always insisted he would become. Even though he hadn't spoken to his parents in five years, and didn't really miss them, proving them right, rather than wrong, about his ineptitude was not something he looked forward to.

Dan sighed and forced himself to cross the room, sit down with his back to Grace, and fiddle with his bottles and beakers.

Someone had to.

Grace was nearly done entering the data into the computer. Five years of research made a lot of paper. Dan was lucky there'd never been a fire. Everything would have been gone. *Poof!* Sometimes geniuses just weren't the brightest bulbs in the box when it came to common sense.

She didn't think Dan had been taking care of him-self, either. He looked tense, pale, as malnourished as a huge guy could look, which shouldn't surprise her since he forgot to eat all the time and he never seemed to go outside unless he were jogging or chopping wood.

She'd discovered why the man had heavy calluses

on his palms. When a problem nagged him too much he chopped wood—a manly version of crocheting, she assumed. When she'd asked him about the huge pile of split logs behind the lab, he'd mumbled something about a woodstove to offset the cost of air-conditioning. The more Grace learned about Dan, the more she found to like.

But she wondered. Had he always been this driven, or was it just the recent ultimatum that had gotten him so uptight?

Glancing at Dan, Grace found him hunched over his little glass tubes, mumbling. Her heart rolled over and flopped into her stomach every time she caught him muttering like a lunatic and mixing things.

When had she started to fall for him? It could have been at any one of a thousand moments. But the fact remained the same—she wanted Dan Chadwick, and she really shouldn't take him.

The past two weeks had been pure torture. At home, Em and Olaf were in love, and while she was thrilled that two of her favorite people had found happiness with each other, watching them make out all the time played havoc with her self-control.

Every morning she worked in Dan's lab. She could hear him; she could see him; she could smell him. She became a model of efficiency trying to keep from staring at him. Since she'd had that talk with Em, all sorts of things were becoming obvious. Dan was not the man she'd thought him to be—he was a whole lot more.

Every night she dreamed of him. Amazingly erotic dreams she'd never believed herself capable of. She would awake hot, damp and unsatisfied, with memories of Dan's mouth on her body and his body on hers.

In her life there'd been one other man. He had been her first, and when she'd discovered his betrayal, she'd vowed he would be her last, too.

Silly thought, she realized now, but she'd had it just the same. All the bad things in her life had converged and she'd had neither the time nor the desire to mess with affairs of the heart again. Then Dan had walked naked into her life. And she had both desire and a mess on her hands.

Every day when she entered the lab, she wanted nothing more than to see him naked again, to touch that big, hard body, to taste that soft, smooth skin. And because she wanted those things so badly, she made herself stare at the computer screen like a robot.

The more she forced herself to work, the more interested in Dan's work she became. The more she read his notes, the more she learned of the man. He was devoted to this project. He believed curing one infection could cure countless more—and he was probably right.

His muttering became louder, and she glanced at him again. So earnest and scientific, he'd run his fingers through his hair until the strands stuck up like corn husks waving in the autumn wind. He hadn't gotten a haircut yet, and he headed into ponytail territory. What would he say if she walked up behind him, smoothed her fingers through that hair, over his neck, down his shoulders and underneath his lab coat?

Grace stifled a moan. She had it bad.

Dan cursed beneath his breath, causing Grace to frown. He never did that. Things must not be going well. She suspected he worked harder than usual these days because of the time limit imposed by Mrs. Cabilla. Because if Dan worked this hard, all the time, he was going to die very young.

Just like her father.

A tiny cry escaped Grace's lips and Dan glanced her way. She jumped up from the computer and crossed the room. He tensed as she approached, as if he expected her to break all his precious beakers. Her mouth twitched. Sometimes she wanted to break them.

She stopped a foot away and held out her hand. Confusion evident upon his face, Dan took her hand. She tugged. He sat there like a lump. She sighed. Spontaneous man, he was not.

"Come with me. There's something you need to see."

"But—"

"No buts." She stepped closer. Close enough to feel his heat and let him feel hers. Holding his gaze with her own, she raised his hand to her lips and placed a kiss on the back. His shiver showed he was as aware of her as she was of him.

While he stared at her mouth, she unbuckled his watch, then her own. "And where we're going, we won't be needing these."

She tossed them onto the table with the rest of the stress-related items and tugged his hand again. This time he stood, though he cast a longing look back at his watch.

"But—"

"Today forget all the buts in your life." She released his hand and unbuttoned his lab coat. His breath caught on a sexy sigh that caused her own body to heat. She needed to stop thinking of sex every time he entered the room. Perhaps if they weren't in a room, the allure would be less. She intended to find out.

Grace shoved the pristine coat from his broad shoulders and let the garment fall to the floor. Dan made a grab for it, but she caught his hands with her own. "Let it go," she whispered. "Let me show you a place where nothing else matters but the blue of the sky and the sun on the water. Just for today, let's be free."

His face torn between hope and uncertainty, he shook his head as he pulled her closer and nuzzled her hair. Grace's heart fell, but the word that brushed her cheek was . . .

"Yes."

Dan had never played hooky in his life. Not in college, not in med school, not from work. Never.

Perhaps that was why he kept looking over his shoulder as he and Grace walked hand in hand out of the cabin. No one shouted, "Stop, thief of time! Get back in there and work!"

So he kept going. He hadn't called Grace the Pied Piper for nothing. When she spoke his name, the music of her voice drew him wherever she led.

They got into her car, and she drove in the opposite direction from town, out into the wilderness,

where he'd never been before. Dan got even more
nervous. What was it he was supposed to do if he
got lost?

Oh, yeah. Hug a tree.

He stared at the miles and miles of evergreens
that looked exactly the same. Sure. That ought to
work.

Without his watch Dan felt adrift. He must have
been insane to let her take it away. But when she'd
come so close her scent invaded his senses, then
kissed his hand and taken off his lab coat, his poor
tired brain had only held one word.

Yes, yes, and yes again.

Well, how long could it take to show him one little
place? What could it hurt to take a few hours off?
Perhaps a few hours was just what he needed.

His granny had always said, "a watched pot never
boils," so the experiment he'd been playing with for
the last several months, which he'd set to boil then
cool, would be fine without him staring at it. He'd
be back by late afternoon and hopefully there'd be
a breakthrough awaiting him.

The lull of the car, the heat of the day, the rolling
miles of highway and acres upon acres of tall, tall
trees made his eyes heavy. Dan awoke when the car
stopped.

"Wh-where are we?"

"Paradise."

"Huh?" Dan peered out the window. A secluded
lake surrounded by trees, a raft floating in the middle, and a rowboat on the shore. "Looks like an
advertisement for Outdoorsmen 'R Us."

"If you're making jokes, you must feel better."

"I felt fine."

"That's why you aren't eating and you look like you haven't slept in a week."

Dan blushed, remembering why he couldn't sleep. "I sleep fine."

"If that were true then you wouldn't have crashed like a baby as soon as I hit the highway."

He ignored her and got out of the car. Leaning his rump against the hood, he stared at the scene. Grace was right. Here the sky was bluer than blue, not a cloud, not a streak of jet stream. Nothing but sky. The sun shone on the pristine water so brightly his eyes ached.

Grace joined him. "See? Doesn't this just make you want to stay here forever?"

He nodded. "What time is it?"

A startled laugh escaped her. "That's all you can say? 'What time is it?' "

"Well, what time is it?"

"I have no idea. I don't time my time off."

Dan glanced at the sky, but he'd never been able to judge the time from the sun—especially when the sun was so high and he had no idea which way was north, south, east or west. He'd never needed to tell the time that way, since he hadn't taken off his watch since . . . since . . . 1981.

He pointed at the sky. "What does the sun say?"

"How would I know?"

"You can't tell the time from the sun?"

"Sorry." She strode off toward the lake.

Dan found himself distracted by the sight of Grace's legs and the shape of her rear in shorts. She hardly ever wore shorts. Just those long, slitted skirts that drove him mad. The shorts had the same effect.

At the lake's edge she struggled to pull the boat from the shore into the water. Dan hurried over and gave her a hand. "You truly don't know what time it is?"

She straightened, put her hands on her hips and shot him that look that plainly said, *Idiot.* But when she spoke her voice was gentle, and he wondered just what in the hell was going on. "No, Dan, I don't know what time it is. I only wear a watch when I'm working, never when I play, and I don't know how to tell time by *giizis.*"

"*Giizis?*"

"The sun. I never learned, because I never cared. By my calculations . . ." She got into the boat. "It's daytime. Are you coming?"

"Coming?"

She raised an eyebrow at him. The word had sounded sexual, though he hadn't meant for it to. Luckily she let it pass without a quip. "On the lake with me. Come out and play, Doctor. It'll be fun."

"But—"

"Ah." She silenced him. "Push off and jump in. Please?"

Why couldn't he relax for just a little while? All he'd wanted for the past two weeks was to touch her again. Today he might get a chance, if only to hold her hand. He could work all night and make up the time.

In answer, Dan shoved the boat the last few inches into the water and stepped in. The boat wobbled alarmingly, and Grace grabbed his hand and yanked him down. Their knees bumped, and her smile blossomed. "I don't suppose you know how to row?"

He glanced at the oars resting inside the boat. How hard could it be? Just once he wanted to know something she thought he should know. "No problem."

In the act of pulling the oars loose from their mooring, she paused to gape at him. "You've rowed before?"

On a rowing machine. "Sure."

"You're elected then." She handed him the oars. "Let's just go out in the middle and drift awhile."

"All right." He fiddled the oars into position with a lot of clunking and thumping, but he made it. Grace watched him with a half smile upon her face.

"Relax. We're all alone. The lake is ours. Peace awaits."

"You're sure no one will show up with a motor boat or jet skies?"

She wrinkled her nose as if she'd smelled something foul. "Not on my lake."

"You own a lake?" He'd gotten the impression she was poor and struggling.

"My mother does—or at least all the land access. Dad bought this place for a vacation retreat. They were going to build a house on the shore and come here on the weekends, maybe retire here, too." She stared past his shoulder with a wistful gaze in her eyes. "You know they never came here once? My dad worked weekends—always. He kept saying next weekend, next summer, next year."

Dan couldn't imagine his mother sitting still for that. But then his mother and father would never plan a weekend retreat, never dream of taking time together, away from their jobs, never, ever allow someone to steal their watch. "And what did your mom say?"

Grace brought her gaze back to him. "She said, 'Yes, darling, whatever you want. Next year is fine with me.' But there wasn't a next year. There will never be a next year for them. My mom *hates* this place now."

Silence fell between them, heavy and still. Dan didn't like to see her sad. She so rarely was. He picked up the oars and started rowing toward the center of the lake. If he could give Grace one thing, he could give her this day, without complaint, without constraint.

"You *can* row."

The surprise in her voice made him frown. "I can do a few things besides mix and stir, read and write."

"I wondered."

Since she smiled when she said it, Dan smiled, too. The sun warmed his muscles. The black T-shirt he'd slipped on that morning as the only thing left clean was probably not the best choice for a late August day on a lake. He set the oars up and pulled the shirt off.

His hair brushed his neck and fell in his eyes. He wished for a moment he had a rubber band to pull the strands out of his face and off of his neck. Then he gave a snort of laughter. Dr. Daniel Chadwick with a ponytail. The image wasn't all that bad.

"What?" Grace asked.

He shook his hair out of the way and discovered her staring at his biceps. He glanced down to discover that rowing made them flex and release. Not bad for a geeky scientist. He looked at Grace again. The expression on her face had Dan's temperature rising several more degrees. "Uh, my hair," he fumbled. "I should get it cut."

"You think?" She lifted her gaze from his arms to his eyes. "I kind of like it."

"You do?" Was that the first time she'd said she liked something about him? Or was it merely the first time he could recall anyone saying they liked anything about him—except his incredible brain, of course.

"I do. If you pull it back when you work, it'll stay out of your eyes."

He nodded, imagining his mother's face if she saw her son wearing a ponytail. The image was too appealing to deny.

"Look." Grace pointed at the sky. The movement pulled her shirt up, baring her midriff. Dan caught a glimpse of tanned, supple skin, stretched over a flat belly. Sweat trickled down the middle of his chest. "Doc!" He looked at her face. Exasperation filled her eyes. "You're going to miss it." She jabbed her finger at the sky again. Her shirt rode higher. She wasn't wearing a bra.

He swallowed the scalding lust at the back of his throat and followed the direction of her hand. A bird soared above the lake, a very big bird. Dan squinted against the flare of the sun.

"Is that . . . ?"

"An eagle. Yes. There's a nest here."

Dan stopped rowing and stared. The boat drifted

on in a lulling, soothing coast across the center of the lake. "I've never seen one," he whispered.

"Never?"

"Never."

"There's a lot you've missed."

"Yes." He tore his gaze from the majestic bird that soared and dipped as if dancing in the sky. The eagle, a symbol of freedom throughout the world, was the perfect image for this day of Grace. Dan lowered his head to look at her.

She stared again. No one had ever gazed at his body with such longing before. Everywhere her eyes touched he burned.

"I *have* missed a lot."

Her gaze flicked from an ardent perusal of his belly, up to his face. The sun had kissed her nose, just a hint of spice on cinnamon skin. Dan wanted to kiss her nose, too. He wanted to kiss a whole lot more than her nose.

Their eyes caught and held. He read desire in the depths of her brown gaze. She licked her lips. "Grace, you make me crazy."

Those lips curved; temptation's name was still Grace. "You don't do so bad at that yourself, Doctor."

She leaned forward and ran a single finger down the center of his chest along the trickle of moisture, the softness of her skin and the rasp of her nail a contrast that had him shivering despite the summer sun. He burned; he froze; he ached. He had to kiss those curving lips or explode.

Leaning forward, Dan puckered up. Grace's eyes drifted closed, a soft sigh of expectation and surrender filled the air, competing with the lap of the waves against the boat.

He couldn't reach her. Frustration filled him. The first time they were alone in the world, no Olaf would come to kill him, and he couldn't reach her for a kiss. Thinking only of those lips on his, Dan stood so he could sit next to Grace on the bench seat and take her into his arms.

The boat tottered. "Uh-oh," Dan murmured, trying to backtrack.

Grace's eyes snapped open. "Ah, hell," she said.

They both went into the water.

scent filled the air, competing with the tang of the water again at the boat.

He couldn't watch her. Frustration filled him[?] that once they were alone in the cabin, he would come to kill him, as He couldn't reach her for a few. Thinking only of those her on his, that anger as he could at least to Grace on the path and and bide his time job strip.

The boat moved. "What?" Dan murmured, coming to put himself

Grace's eyes snapped open. "Ah, well," she said. "I had such wonderful water."

Thirteen

Grace couldn't help but laugh as she went into the water. That's how she ended up with a mouthful of lake. She came up coughing, and sputtering, and gagging. By the time she cleared her throat, her teeth tasted like seaweed.

Her heart gave a sharp, panicked kick when her searching gaze did not discover Dan. *Dear God, please let him be able to swim.*

She hadn't thought to ask. What adult couldn't swim these days? Probably quite a few. But what kind of lunatic would go on a boat without putting on a life jacket if they couldn't swim? Double quite a few.

"Dan!" she shouted, preparing to dive.

"Here." His voice came from the other side of the boat. The breath she held blew past her lips in a rush that shook in the middle.

Since he wasn't dead, she just might kill him.

His face appeared around the end. "You okay?"

"As soon as I kill you I'll be fine." She kicked her feet to stay afloat, and one of her sandals went to the bottom of the lake.

"Sorry." He sounded sheepish. "I wasn't thinking." He held out a hand and drew her toward the boat.

"With your brain anyway."

"You had the same idea."

True enough. Watching him row half-naked had made her half-crazy. Perhaps a dunk in the lake had been the best thing for both of them, although her body still thrummed with awareness as they treaded water hip-to-hip.

"Guilty as charged," she admitted.

"Now what?"

"Want to go swimming?"

"Do I have a choice?"

"No. We're close enough to the raft to pull the boat over and get back in from there."

"We can't get in from here?"

"You ever try to get back into a boat without a ladder or help from the inside?"

"No."

"Believe me, it's easier to swim a few yards and get back in from the raft. Grab the mooring line."

Grace led the way. Dan hauled the boat, no easy trick while swimming. The more she knew of Dan, the more surprised Grace became at how little she knew him at all.

Minutes later they reached the raft and Grace hauled herself up the ladder. Even though she wore only shorts, a tank top, and one shoe, sopping wet clothes could be amazingly heavy. She grabbed the shorts to keep them from sliding down her legs and back into the lake.

Dan emerged from the water looking like a Norse god. Her mouth went dry. Water streamed down the muscles of his bare chest, glistening in the early afternoon sun. His hair had darkened from the damp yet still glowed golden. His shorts, cut-off sweatpants from the looks of them, left little to the imagination when wet. And Grace had more than a little imagination. Her hands itched to run all over him.

He secured the mooring line with a deft twist, turned, and found her drooling over him. His grin made her knees wobble.

"I think we'd better rest here awhile." Her cheeks heated when her voice came out sounding like an advertisement for 1-900-SEX-4YOU. Forgetting how small a raft was, especially with a man the size of a football player aboard, she turned around too fast, lost her balance and windmilled her arms to keep from going back into the drink. Dan's firm, strong hands on her shoulders saved her. The warmth of his hands put her at peril once more.

Though the day was hot, the breeze wasn't; its whisper made her shiver. Together they stood on the raft in the middle of a deserted lake, the sunshine beating down, the eagles dancing somewhere in the distance, and neither seemed to know what to do, what to say, next.

Grace expected Dan to turn her in his arms so he could kiss her again. Or maybe he would just press that clever mouth to her neck, then work his way down. Maybe he wouldn't kiss her at all, maybe he would touch her—where she wanted him to touch her the most.

Shifting at that thought, her nipples, hardened from the cool, clear water, slid along the inside of her shirt. The sensation, coming so quickly on the heels of salacious thoughts, made her body flood with desire.

Yes, her mind whispered, *touch me there, touch me every-everywhere.*

But when he broke the hovering, sizzling tension between them, he did none of the things her mind and body begged for. Instead he yanked the band from her braid and ran his fingers through the wet length, gently, almost reverently, never pulling, never tugging, releasing the heavy mass from its twisted confines to flop heavy along her back.

He bent and buried his face in the strands, rubbing his cheek like a cat. Grace shuddered. How could such a simple thing as touching her hair be so unbelievably arousing?

When he shifted his hands from her shoulders to her waist, then along her bare belly, the calluses on his fingers scraped the muscles that twitched and tightened beneath her skin. His mouth at her ear, he whispered, "Grace?"

"Mmm?"

"Can I touch you?"

In answer, she pressed herself to his bare chest, the desire to feel his taut, muscled skin against her own made her want to rip off her wet T-shirt, but she restrained herself—from that, anyway. Instead she molded her body to his hardness, arched her back and begged him without words to touch her and more.

His palms skimmed up her rib cage; he filled his hands with her breasts—almost. His thumbs teased her; his fingers stroked her. Her head fell back, resting on his chest, and she wasn't sure, but she thought he kissed the top of her head. Desire and tenderness warred within her.

Once she'd said there could be nothing like this between them. Stupid of her. This *was* between them and it wasn't going to go away. She didn't want to like him. She didn't want to want him. She really, really didn't want to love him.

Her mind skittered away from serious thoughts as her body pulled her into the abyss of awareness that had stretched between them from the very beginning. She had to feel his skin against hers.

Pulling away from his gentle touches, she turned in his arms and put her hands against his chest. Holding his gaze with her own, she traced well-defined muscles with trained fingertips, pressed the heel of her hand against bone, ran her thumb along the ridges of his belly and ribs, then dipped into the valley at his navel. His eyes darkened with desire, and when he tugged on the hem of her shirt, she raised her arms over her head in mute agreement.

He slid the shirt over her arms and with a wink flipped it over his shoulder. The sound of the garment *plotch*ing into the lake froze his cocky smile.

Throwing her shirt into the water in the middle of seducing her was so Dan that Grace had to giggle. The horrified look on his face dissolved when she said, "Oops," and flipped her palms open in a careless gesture. His smile was reward for a thousand misdemeanors.

She forgot them all when his clever fingers followed the path her shirt had taken, all the way back down, sliding over her arms, her rib cage, her hips. She lowered her hands to his shoulders and rubbed her breasts along his chest, the intimate contact only inflaming her further.

His quick intake of breath and the flex of his hips showed he enjoyed the first meeting of flesh on flesh as much as she did. He lowered his head, but bypassed her lips and instead, honed in on the ridge of muscle that joined her neck and shoulder. His teeth grazed her skin, his tongue laved the sting, his lips suckled her into his mouth, and she moaned wanting more, more, more.

Fingertips ran along the waistband of her shorts, dipped beneath the line of her panties, then lowered everything, inch by inch. Soon she would be stark naked beneath the sun. Hmm, that had possibilities.

"Wait," she said.

He froze, sighed, then slowly pulled her clothes back around her waist and buried his nose in her hair.

"Sorry," he mumbled. "I wasn't thinking."

He straightened and the disappointment in his eyes made her heart turn over. Why did she think everything he did was so damned cute?

"I didn't say stop," she reminded him. "I just said wait."

Confusion spread over his face, making him look like a lost, little boy, and ten times cuter than he'd looked a minute ago. She shook her head, took his hand, and pulled him over to the small wooden box attached to the corner of the raft. She knelt and opened the lid, pulled out a sealed, plastic bag, and took the blanket from inside. A flick of her wrists and the hard wooden floor of the raft was covered.

"Not the Taj Mahal but at least I won't get slivers," she said.

Slipping her thumbs into her waistband, she dropped her pants to the ground and stepped free. It had been far too long since she'd stood naked beneath the sun, and for a moment she just let the air warm her and the breeze caress her.

When she sat on the blanket and glanced at Dan she found him staring at her as if she were some foreign and exotic creature he might frighten if he moved too fast. His gaze wandered over her, causing heat without benefit of touch. He seemed punch-drunk, poor man.

"Dan?"

"Mmm?"

"Get undressed and come here."

His eyes flicked from her legs to her face. She lay back and held out her arms. To his credit, he didn't ogle, but continued to hold her gaze.

"You're sure?" he asked.

She smiled. "Just don't throw your pants in the lake."

He didn't.

His body blotted out the sheen of the sun. His weight pressed her into the blanket, warmed by the wood beneath her back. His scent, man and lake and lime aftershave, surrounded her, filled her with a strange emotion—frantic desire and immense tenderness. Wherever his skin met hers she ached; she burned. No touch stopped the pain, no kiss soothed the fire. She liked it that way.

Fulfilling her every fantasy, she stroked him with her fingers, molded him along the heart of her palms, discovered every curve and dip. She buried her face in the curls that dusted his belly, rubbed her cheek along the contrast of hard muscle and soft hair, filled her lungs with the scent of his skin, and her mouth with the essence of him. With her hands she gathered him close, with her lips she adored, with her tongue she tasted.

Dan was a banquet and Grace a starving woman. She had not known how hungry her life had been until he knocked on her door and barged into her undernourished life.

His desire as ravenous as her own, she fed his hunger with her body, quenched his thirst at her lips. She did not feel satiated until he filled her emptiness, and his cry of release echoed her name.

Dan came back to himself because the sun was burning his butt. He didn't have skin made for outdoor, daytime romps in the nude. But to experience again what he'd just experienced in the circle of Grace's arms, within the gentle warmth of her body, he would risk Hell itself.

For sex? his conscience mocked.

What had just happened had not been just sex. He'd had sex—not a lot, but he'd had it—and this had not been just sex. This had been . . .

What?

A life-altering, mind-bending, world-changing . . . something.

His spectacular brain couldn't seem to come up with an adequate word to describe the meeting of body, mind, and soul that had just overtaken him. Had Grace felt it, too?

He started to withdraw, afraid he might crush her, but long, supple legs clenched about his waist, holding him right where he was. His body jerked in response and she chuckled, low in her throat, the vibrations rumbling along his chest, making him want to nuzzle her hair, kiss her ear, crawl right inside her and stay warm forever.

"Shh," she murmured, running her fingers through the hair at the nape of his neck, making him want to purr and cuddle. "Don't go."

"Where would I go?" He lifted his head so he could see her face.

She smiled, though her eyes remained closed, then rocked against him, the muscles of her inner walls tightening, making him hard far too soon to be believed. "Don't *go*," she repeated. Her eyes opened, and he tumbled into their dark depths. "Stay right here with me."

"Okay."

He was incapable of denying her anything right now. Probably incapable of denying her anything ever again.

So he didn't deny her or himself. They romped once more beneath the sun, above the water. She whispered words in a multitude of languages, the exotic endearments enflaming him. His name breathed past her lips, over and over in English made him grin as he pressed his lips to her neck. She definitely knew who he was.

Slowly, achingly, he moved within her. Gently, easily, he took her with him over the edge one more time for good measure. To heck with sunburn, his body and soul were on fire with the miracle he and Grace made together.

Later, much later, when they lay side by side, holding hands and watching the clouds, Dan experienced the greatest peace he'd ever known. What could be better than lying beneath the sun with a woman like Grace?

Lying beneath the sun after having great sex twice with Grace.

Suddenly, panic rocked him and the peace he'd searched for all his life fled. What had he done? Where was his brain? Not functioning when he needed it the most. Disentangling himself from her despite her mumbled protests, Dan sat up and cast a frantic glance about. There! There they were! He grabbed his pants, yanked out his wallet, and scrambled madly for—

"What are you trying to find?"

He glanced at her. She sat up, staring at him in sleepy confusion, so at ease with her nakedness, her skin a luscious golden-bronze, shimmering beneath the summer sun. His mind went numb, and he just stared, wanting her all over again.

She snapped her fingers in front of his face. "What do you have there, Doc?"

He held up an unopened foil packet, unable to speak for the horror.

She looked at it for a moment, then returned her unfathomable gaze to his. She shrugged. "Oops."

"Oops? Oops? All you can say is oops? This is serious, Grace. And all my fault." He put his free hand to his forehead and rubbed the burgeoning ache.

'I'm sorry. I've had this thing in my wallet for years. I've never been very good at suave and debonair maneuvers."

"Thank God."

"Huh?" He dropped his hand.

"Suave and debonair is not my type. Relax, Dan. I've got the pregnancy issue covered."

"You do?"

"I may be free-spirited, but I'm not an idiot. And no, I don't sleep around. You would be the . . ." She tapped her lip with her finger ". . . second guy I've slept with in this lifetime." Before he could question that little tidbit, she continued. "From the age of that condom, it looks like you don't sleep around either, so we have the other issue covered."

Dan hung his head so she wouldn't see him blush. Such frank talk embarrassed him. He just wasn't a gigolo.

She scooted closer so they bumped hips. Her hand slid along his arm, and her fingers laced with his. "Hey, how come a hunk like you has a prehistoric condom?"

"Hunk?" Dan's head came up and he stared at her, amazed. "Me?"

"Yes, you. Don't tell me girls with glasses haven't been hanging on your arm since you put out your doctor shingle."

"Uh, not exactly."

"It's okay. You can tell me."

"Quit teasing, Grace. I'm not much of a stud muffin."

She squeezed his hand. "You are to me."

He stared into her eyes for a long moment. She

looked serious. He'd have to think about that. *Later.* Right now he had questions of his own. "Why would a woman like you be alone so long?"

Her face, which had been open and smiling, suddenly became shuttered and sad. "Because of how I look."

"You lost me."

"Guys think it would be exotic to date an Indian. Hey, savages must be wild in bed, right?"

Dan winced. How crude. "Who thinks that?"

"Never mind. The fact is most men don't want to date *me*. They're interested in my face or fascinated with the color of my skin. Which is it for you, Dan?"

If he hadn't caught the need in her eyes and the vulnerable tremble of her mouth, he would have been insulted. Someone had hurt her badly. He wanted to take them apart with his bare hands. Suddenly Olaf's anger at him made a lot of sense. The only thing Dan could do to heal her pain was to ensure he didn't hurt her again. He'd merrily let Olaf tear an arm out of the socket if that happened.

"I'm not saying you aren't exotic." She turned away, staring out at the lake. "That's the first thing I noticed when I saw you step around that oriental screen. I'm not going to apologize because I thought you were the most beautiful woman I'd ever seen. But I told you once you have a Ferrari inside, Grace, and I meant that. I quit seeing your face the second time I saw you."

He cupped her cheek in his palm and turned her face so he could look into those deep, dark eyes.

"So what do you see now?" she whispered.

"I only see the you behind those eyes."

Her smile lit up the sky at dusk. Her kiss made him forget something he suddenly needed to remember. A long while later, that something came to him.

The sun was setting. The day was through.

His experiment was ruined.

Fourteen

Dan shot up from the raft like a rocket and started getting dressed, muttering to himself in a distracted, panicked litany that made Grace nervous. Had too much sun and extremely great sex fried his incredible brain?

He didn't even bother to tell her what was wrong. He just finished dressing and got into the boat, murmuring something that sounded like "Rebellion is bad."

Grace sat on the blanket and watched him get ready to leave her in the middle of a great big nowhere. Had she really thought his absentminded muttering cute?

"Hey, Doc, where do you think you're going?"

"Huh?" He glanced up from his panicked fumbling with the oars, blinked at her as if she were a shocking surprise, and scowled. "Grace, get dressed. It's nearly dark."

"There aren't any vampires around here. And the bats won't bother us. What's wrong with the dark?"

"I have to get back. What time is it?"

"Nighttime." She stood and wrapped the blanket around herself.

"What are you doing? Get dressed."

"That's a little hard since my shirt is gone, and my shoe is at the bottom of the lake. I think my shorts shrunk. I'll have to wear this home." She twisted the blanket into a sarong.

"Whatever. Just hurry."

She climbed into the boat and Dan took off rowing before she settled onto the seat. "What's the rush?"

"My experiment. I should have been home hours ago. I might still save it if I can get there in the next half hour."

"Uh-oh."

Dan stopped rowing, and the boat drifted toward shore. "Don't say 'Uh-oh.'"

"All right." Grace's heart had started a panic dance of its own. What had she done?

"Say something!"

"Oops?"

Dan groaned. "Spill it."

"We're in Minnesota."

"What?" The single word echoed across the lake. Grace winced. "You were sleeping all the way here. I drove for two hours."

He started laughing. He'd definitely blown a brain watt. "Very funny. You had me going."

"I'm serious."

He stopped laughing. "Damn."

He began to row, but more slowly this time. The lack of panic scared Grace more than the panic had. "Dan, say something."

"What is there to say? I'm not even surprised. This is what happens when I rebel. All my life, every time

I tried to do something a little bit different, disaster followed."

She didn't like the way he said "do something different." He'd just done her, and she'd always been different. "You don't seem the rebellious type."

"My entire career is a great big rebellion. And now it's a disaster, too. You think I would have learned my lesson by now. This just proves I learned nothing."

"What do you mean by 'this?' I took you away for a day. You deserved a break. We both did. I thought this afternoon was more than an interlude and a hell of a lot more than a little rebellion. Or was I wrong?"

The bottom of the boat scraped the shore and Dan hopped out. He held out his hand to her, but she ignored him. A different sort of panic had settled in her heart. Had she been wrong about Dan? Was what they had shared during this golden afternoon merely a little walk on the wild side for the good Dr. Chadwick? She found that hard to believe, but she'd been suckered before by a man like him.

He walked toward the car, mumbling again, and she didn't press the issue. She had issues of her own, thank you.

The drive home was as silent as the drive there had been, but for different reasons. When she stopped in front of the lab, Dan was out of the car and running into the cabin before she could turn off the engine. Grace sat for a long moment staring at the light in the window. Should she stay or should she go? The continued silence from the cabin unnerved her, and she could not just drive away without knowing the truth, or discovering the lie.

He sat where he always did—on a stool at the center island table—but he looked different. Was it because he wore a wrinkled black shirt and no lab coat? Perhaps the bare feet instead of shiny shoes? No, it was the dejected slump of the shoulders instead of the lighthearted movements that usually characterized his mixing and mumbling.

She didn't speak; she didn't move, but he knew she was there because he spoke. "Trashed. Wrecked. Ruined. Crap." He gave a short bark of laughter that didn't sound amused. Grace didn't feel like laughing either. "Months of work because I took an afternoon off. You win, Grace."

"Win what?"

"The whole shebang. The big banana. The grant. The money."

She'd forgotten. Silly of her. All she'd been thinking about was him. "Who says I win? Who says I want to?"

"This fiasco sets me back at least a year. So I give up, and you win. Your blankie-drop will be funded. And why shouldn't it be? Isn't that what these last few weeks have been about?"

"Is it? If that's what you think, then you don't know me at all."

Her cool tone must have penetrated his misery because he turned slowly toward her as she stalked across the distance that separated them. "Sure I want the grant. But not at your expense. Tell me why this is so important to you? Tell me why you're willing to give up a normal life, your health, your happiness for . . . for . . . for whatever the hell it is you want to cure so badly."

"Because thousands of people—"

She held up her hand. "No more propaganda, Dan. Tell me the truth."

For a moment she thought he'd put her off with more drivel. Then he gave a quick nod and spilled it. "My parents were very disappointed in me when I chose this profession."

"Medical research? I'd think they'd be thrilled and very proud."

"You'd think. But they said I was wasting myself in research. Truth is, I'm a coward. People make me nervous."

"I've never noticed that about you. Except with Olaf and he makes everyone nervous."

"I feel comfortable with you and the Jewels. More comfortable than I've ever felt with anyone. Even my family. People in pain—all that emotion, focused on me, I didn't cope well."

"Maybe that's because you care too much. What's the crime in that?"

He flicked a glance at her from beneath his bangs, and his face revealed he'd never thought of that before. "I don't understand."

"You care, Dan. I saw you with Em. I've seen you with your work. It wouldn't obsess you so much if you didn't truly want to help people. Just because you aren't on the front lines doesn't mean you aren't contributing to the battle. Quit beating yourself up over who you are. Accept it and be proud. So you like bottles and beakers. Big deal. Someone has to."

His smile was a shadow of the grin she'd come to crave, but at least he wasn't hanging his head anymore. "I do like being alone with my stuff. My sister, the cardiothoracic surgeon, calls me Dr. Frankenstein."

"How—cute." Grace wanted to smack his sister up alongside her head.

"I think my parents would have adjusted if I'd gone to work for one of the big research hospitals and put my brilliance to use curing cancer. But I've never been interested in taking the usual path. I chose an underdog disease."

"Because you're an underdog."

He shrugged. "I truly believe that by finding out why a minor infection occurs you can prevent all kinds of major infections. But my parents were embarrassed. Toenail fungus isn't very glamorous. They told me I was wasting my brilliance."

"Wasting! You blaze trails from nothing. Why don't they try it?"

He looked at her like she were some new bug he would like to stick on a pin and put beneath his microscope. Obviously what she thought was big news to him. "At any rate, they disinherited me. I haven't spoken to them in five years."

"Good riddance," Grace muttered.

Dan lifted an eyebrow and his lips twitched. Progress. "I thought if I could make a success of this I'd prove my theory and win them over. But once again—disaster." The smile dissolved and Grace wanted to kiss those sad, sad lips.

He turned around again and pushed the glass jar with the "crap" in it across the table with his finger.

His sigh was long and deep, and wavered in the middle. Grace lost the battle. She had to touch him.

Leaning against his back, she slid her arms around his neck and snuggled her head along his shoulder. He tensed but didn't shrug her off.

"Maybe you started out wanting to prove your parents wrong, but I think somewhere along the line you discovered you wanted to help the suffering masses more. Forget about the insufferable messes that pretended to be family."

His snort of laughter warmed her soul. When he put his hands over hers, their joined fingers lay over his heart. "Stay with me tonight, Grace. I need you more than I've ever needed anyone or anything."

She shouldn't.

Grace opened her mouth to explain, and "yes" whispered past her lips. With no more words left, Dan carried her to his cabin.

They both smelled of lake water and waning sunshine. Dan would have liked to take Grace directly to his bed. He'd imagined her there so many times. Instead he took a detour to the shower.

Luckily his cabin previously had been the camp director's, so he had his own bathroom. While showering with Grace in the community showers might have sparked adolescent fantasies, he'd been having enough of those lately and he really needed to get over it.

Dan kicked open the door of his cabin and crossed the crowded room. He set Grace down at the bathroom door. She glanced over his shoulder at the bed, then back at him in confusion.

"You want to use the shower?"

"Are you saying I smell?"

"I just thought—" He shrugged.

"Oh!" She smiled seductively, which confused his mind, but his body went hot all over, even though his skin was chilled from driving two hours in wet pants. "I get it. Shower. Sure."

Dan didn't get it, until she yanked the tie on her blanket sarong and the material dropped to the floor with a damp-sounding thud.

"Let's take a shower."

"Let's? As in us?"

"Don't sound so surprised. I thought that's what you wanted."

Pathetic as it was to admit, and he didn't plan on admitting it, Dan had never taken a shower with anyone else. Except in a locker room, and that really didn't count.

"Of course that's what I want," he blurted, afraid she might change her mind if he stood there gawking for too long.

But who wouldn't stare at the beauty of Grace. Her skin was the same shade all over and smooth as honey. Except there, where she had a scrape on her belly and there an odd-shaped mark on her hip, and was that a bruise on her thigh?

She'd turned to precede him into the bathroom, but he caught her arm. "What's this?" He traced his thumb along her hipbone.

Her breath caught and she leaned into his touch.

That movement—sensual, yet trusting, made Dan's own breath catch.

Grace glanced down and so did he. The sight of his lighter hand against her darker hip made him think of an artsy black-and-white photograph. He spread his large fingers around her small waist, fascinated with the texture of her skin and the contrast in the shades.

"I think that's from your teeth."

He lost all interest in art and color as his gaze flew up to hers, and he snatched his hand away as if she'd slapped him. He wanted to slap himself. "God, Grace, I'm sorry."

"I'm not." She drew his hand back to her stomach and held him there. "You want to make a matching set?"

"Yep." The word was out before he realized it. Grace laughed, probably from sight of the shock on his face.

"Come on then." She pulled him after her into the small bathroom, undressing him like he was a sick child.

Dan couldn't seem to function very well. Sadness danced in his belly to the drumbeat of the need he had for Grace. She was trying to keep things light, to get his mind off his failure. And as she dropped the last stitch of his clothes into a pile on floor, his mind stopped thinking about anything other than this tiny room that was starting to fill with steam.

Grace stepped into the tiny shower stall. Dan stood there like a lump and hoped he didn't start to drool as she threw back her head and let the water flow down her face and neck, then cascade over her cinnamon-tipped breasts. She turned her head and smiled at him through the foggy glass door. Beads of water dotted her face and her eyelashes were clumped together in such a way that her eyes looked even darker than usual, if that were possible.

"Are you coming, Dan?"

Not yet, he thought. "Soon."

She raised a brow. "How soon?"

"Aren't you the one who told me to stop and smell the coffee?"

"Coffee?"

"Relax, Juan Valdez, it's just an expression."

"Too bad. I'd like some coffee."

"Later. After."

"Come on in here and show me before."

He gave a long-suffering sigh. "All right. If I must, I must."

The shower stall had never seemed big, especially for a man of Dan's size. But with Grace in there too, it suddenly seemed just right. He couldn't move without bumping into her.

She picked up a bottle from the floor. He became distracted by the view so that when she spoke her words didn't register for several seconds. "I've been dying to wash your hair since I first got my hands into it."

He blinked the water from his eyes. "My hair?"

Grinning, Grace poured shampoo into her palm. "Kinky little me, huh?"

She hadn't actually meant they were going to take a washing kind of shower, had she? Knowing Grace, she wanted to conserve natural resources. She hadn't even considered satisfying a fantasy Dan hadn't even known he had.

"Bend down," she ordered. He sighed, and did as he was told.

Grace raised her arms and started massaging his head. Her slick, perfect breasts came level with his face. "Isn't this nice?"

"Huh?"

"I always liked it when my mother washed my hair. I got so relaxed."

Dan was anything but relaxed. He tried to close his eyes so he wouldn't have to look at what he shouldn't touch or taste. But then he could smell her, he could feel her heat, so close to his lips all he had to do was pucker and he would touch them. No, she couldn't be that close, could she?

Tentatively, Dan stretched his mouth outward. A nipple brushed his lips and he captured it. She gasped, but she didn't protest. In fact she arched against him and moaned, then clasped his shoulders when he yanked her closer and set about putting matching marks everywhere she suggested.

Grace had a lot of excellent suggestions.

The one he liked the most was called wash but do not kiss. Dan lathed soap over every exquisite inch of Grace, he looked and he touched but he did not kiss and he did not take. Then she did the same for him. By the time the water ran tepid, they were both hot enough to not care much.

With only a haphazard use of a towel they tumbled from the shower and onto his bed. Dan was in such a state he could think of nothing beyond the feel of her body beneath his. He had to feel her body around his or explode. He drove into her as soon as they landed on the mattress.

She gasped and he froze, afraid he'd hurt her. Idiot. She was tall, but she was fragile. Or more fragile than him. Who wasn't?

"Don't you dare stop." She arched against him. "Don't you dare smell the coffee now, Dan."

He laughed, right in the middle of the most erotic sex he'd ever had. She opened her eyes and grinned.

"Coffee after," he said.

"Long after."

Dan finished what she'd started, and then he started and she finished, then they both started and finished together. They forgot about coffee because there didn't seem to be much after. Only a whole lot of before, during, and again.

Much later, silver slivers of moonlight spilled through the window and across Dan's bed. He wasn't in the bed. Grace was. He'd been sitting in a chair, watching her sleep for at least an hour.

She was the most beautiful thing he'd ever seen, and not because of the shape of her face or the shade of her body, but because she was Grace, and he loved her. He wanted to watch her every day for the rest of his life.

She had not wanted to stay with him; he had seen that in her eyes. Yet she had, because he'd needed her to. He probably should have sent her home, but he hadn't been able to do that once she'd touched him. When Grace touched him, every ache in his life went away.

Was that love? The realization that another person

filled a part of you that you didn't even know was empty?

Dan knew nothing of love. Oh, sure, his parents had loved him, though they'd never said the words. They probably loved each other, too, but it would be inappropriate to act like they did.

Dan had not known he was lonely until Grace came into his life. Now every moment he spent without her rang hollow. Waking up entangled in her arms was the most soul-shattering experience of his life. How was he going to get her to stay with him forever?

He had an idea.

Dan left the cabin with a final, lingering gaze at the woman in his bed before he went to the lab. One last look and then he'd do what he had to do.

Sitting down at his worktable, Dan pulled the jar of crap close and stared morosely into the bottom of his work. He blinked. He straightened. He opened his mouth, shut it again, and then began to laugh. He put his arms onto the table and laid his forehead against them. Then he laughed until tears ran down his face.

A door closed somewhere in the distance. Grace awoke, alone, in a strange bed. Where was Dan?

She found his T-shirt, dropped the garment over her nakedness, hugged the soft cotton that smelled of lake water and him to her skin, then slid from the room. A light in the lab drew her. Was he working again already?

Not wanting to disturb him, Grace looked into

one of the windows. Her heart filled with pain as she watched him look into the jar, then put his head onto the table in a gesture of despair. His shoulders shook as he cried.

Grace blinked away tears of her own. His earnest devotion to what he believed tore at her heart. She'd said they were different from each other, but in many ways they were alike. She could feel his pain as if it were her own.

She took a step toward the back door, meaning to go in and lead him back to bed. She would make him forget everything but them, as she had only a few hours before. But obviously the explosive passion and tender lovemaking they had shared had not been enough to cleanse his heart. Only one thing would do that.

Project Hope was worthy. Project Hope was her baby, her dream. But Dan—Dan was her love.

Lord knows she had tried not to love him. She hadn't even wanted to like him. She'd projected all the bad qualities of men in her past who had betrayed and hurt her. But Dan was not like Jared; he was not like her father. He was Dan—and just as he'd said she had a Ferrari inside—the man had a Cadillac heart.

She had to trust him not to hurt her. She had to trust him to be the man he seemed to be. She had to trust that when he said his research could help countless people, he was telling the truth. A man that would cry because he'd failed at curing toenail fungus was a man she couldn't live without.

Leaving him to his turbulent emotions, Grace returned to Dan's bed. Before she fell back asleep, she made one little phone call that she hoped would fix all the ills of their world.

Unfortunately, she was wrong.

She awoke to an incessant pounding on the door. The sun baked the bed. She'd thrown off all the covers and her clothes. Dan was nowhere in sight.

Grace yanked the sheet from the floor, wrapped it around herself, and opened the door.

The woman on the porch was nearly as surprised to see Grace as Grace was surprised to see her. Early on a sunny morning, and the visitor was dressed to the nines in a pale pink suit, heels, and nylons despite the heat. Her blond hair was fashioned into an expert twist, and an age from that smooth, beautiful face was impossible to determine.

She looked Grace up. She looked Grace down. Her patrician nose wrinkled, then went up in the air. "Who, may I ask, are you?"

Grace disliked her on the spot. Bad habit, but it saved time. Her chin followed the direction of the woman's nose. "Who are you?"

"Penelope Chadwick," she stated, as if Grace should know her name. And Grace had a sinking feeling she should. "Are you Daniel's latest rebellion?"

Grace gripped the door as if she might fall. She wanted to. This was so much worse than Jared walking into her father's funeral with the wife and kiddies. This time Grace got to meet the wife while naked, with the bed of iniquity at her back. She wanted to die right then and there.

But first she would kill Dan. All she had to do was find him.

Fifteen

Dan returned from his errand by ten A.M., and he could barely find a place to park in front of his cabin. The only cars he recognized were Grace's truck and Olaf's boat. The sight of the latter made Dan wince as he got out of his car.

Grace had stayed the night without benefit of matrimony and Olaf would be out for blood. Dan hoped he would get a chance to say he wanted Grace to make an honest man out of him, before Olaf broke his nose.

But who were all these other people?

It didn't take Dan long to find out. As soon as he got out of the car, the mob descended.

The Jewels, Olaf—no surprise—Mrs. Cabilla and Perry, which explained why he hadn't been able to get ahold of them, some gray-haired guy he didn't know and . . . double-damn.

His parents.

"Mother." He nodded. "Father."

"Daniel, who was that woman I found in your room?"

"Nice to see you, too, Mom. How long has it been?"

As usual, his mother ignored both his sarcasm and his question. "She looked Native. I take it she's the latest in your string of rebellious behavior."

Dan narrowed his eyes. "Where is she?"

Suddenly Dan hung several feet above the ground from his collar. "Gracie was in your room? All night long? Bad man, say your prayers."

"What do you think you're doing?" Dan's father demanded. "Put my son down this instant."

Olaf shook Dan like a puppy with a scrap of cloth. "No."

Dan's mother and father looked confused. They did not know what to make of a person who said "no" to them. When the Drs. Chadwick spoke, the world listened and obeyed.

"Olaf, sweetie-pie." Em stepped forward. "Put the doctor down."

Her fuschia peignoir swirled about her ankles. Dan's mother looked as if she'd swallowed an entire cup of lemon juice. Dan would have laughed if Olaf hadn't been choking off his air.

Olaf shook him again. Dan was starting to see stars and hear tweety-birds. "He is a very bad man. He must die. Say bye-bye."

"Babycakes, you promised me when you dragged me out of bed that we would only make sure Grace was all right. No killing before noon."

"A hill beneath the moon?" Garnet shouted.

Dan's mother jumped a foot.

Ruby put an arm around her and said, "Never mind my sister, she eats the dead."

Penelope Chadwick turned green. She would be

quite disconcerted to know the shade did not match her suit.

"Olaf!" Em stamped her foot.

"No, Em. I love you with all my huge heart, but here I draw my line in the mud. He touched Gracie with inappropriateness—a lot. He must die."

"I love her," Dan managed.

Olaf dropped him. Dan hit the ground, hard, and lay there gasping for air as the entire group gathered around, staring at him with varying degrees of differing emotions.

"Love is good," intoned the long-haired man.

"Who the hell are you?" Dan growled.

Mrs. Cabilla appeared next to the stranger. "This is *Abuelo*. My new husband."

"Uh-oh."

Perry's weasel face wove into view, but instead of a sarcastic comment, he shrugged. Life just got weirder and weirder.

Dan was dizzy from all the conflicting subjects, not to mention the lingering effects of strangulation and a head injury, so he just lay where he'd fallen until the world quit revolving.

"Love?" Olaf shouted, loud enough to wake the dead. "Bah! You do not know the word."

Dan needed to sit for this argument. He did, happy to discover the tweety-birds had quit singing, then he looked up, up, up Olaf's monstrous frame and met the man's still-furious eyes. "I do know the meaning of the word. Love means Grace. I mean to marry her."

"Marry? Are you insane, Daniel?" That was his mother.

His father said, "You don't marry them, Dan. Sleep with them, maybe. Marriage never."

"What exactly do you mean by 'them?' "

"Women like this Grace."

Olaf hissed. Em held him back. Dan was almost sorry to see Olaf let her. His parents kept blathering blindly on. Why had he ever cared what they thought?

"Daniel, we came here to make peace. To offer you our support for your work. We've heard about your new project. It has possibilities. But if you insist on continuing with this latest rebellion, I'm afraid we'll have to leave without giving you your check."

Dan stood. "Shove your check, Mummy and Daddy." His mother gasped. His father turned red. "I love Grace. I *will* marry her. The new project you heard about is her project, and I mean to help make the dream come true."

"You're choosing that woman over your family?"

"What family? I haven't spoken to you in five years. I doubt I'll miss you over the next ten. Family means love. Love means—"

"Never having to say you're sorry," *Abuelo* put in.

"That, too. But it also means accepting people as they are, no matter what. Loving them for who they are and not despite it. If you love someone, they don't have to prove themselves worthy. They *are* worthy, just because they are."

"You choose her over your own flesh and blood?"

"You wouldn't know flesh and blood if it bit you on the butt, Mother."

She looked at him as if he'd dropped his pants in the dining room at the country club. "How attractive, Daniel. I should have known that by living with trash, you'd become trash."

Dan did a little "ta-da" shuffle and swept out his arm in a flourish. "And that, ladies and gentleman, is why I live alone."

Everyone laughed but his parents. No surprise there. How had they managed to get through life without a sense of humor? Easy answer. They'd managed, but they had not discovered the joy in life— the joy Grace had given him.

The Chadwicks left without so much as a wave, but then they'd never been much for touchy-feely good-byes. Dan wasn't sorry to see them go. But where was Grace? She'd missed all the fun.

"You know, the money's yours." Perry spoke for the first time. "Miss Lighthorse withdrew her application."

"Well, unwithdraw it."

"Sorry. She says you need the money more than her."

"I don't need the money at all. I thought the entire point of us working together was for one of us to bow out. I'm bowing out."

Perry looked like he'd swallowed something too big for his skinny neck. He looked at Mrs. Cabilla and spread his hands wide.

"What's going on here?" Dan asked.

"I don't know how to explain," Mrs. Cabilla said.

"Try the truth."

She sighed. "Yes, well, um . . . I just wanted you and Grace to find each other. That's why I had Perry give you the ultimatum, set up the conference call, and then leave you stranded at the house."

"Matchmaking?"

"Guilty. But it worked. Perry never thought it would. He said you were too stiff and Grace too free-spirited. But *Abuelo* and I know how opposites attract." She shot a smile filled with adoration at the strange little man who held her hand.

"So Perry dislikes me because I'm stiff, and dislikes Grace because she isn't?"

"Not exactly." She shrugged. "Perry doesn't like anyone but me."

Dan glanced at Perry, but the weaseled one had already retreated out of earshot. "Makes for a sad life."

"I know. I plan to turn my matchmaking skills on him next."

"Good luck," Dan muttered.

"But, Dan, I can't have you giving up on your research, regardless of your love for Grace."

"I'm not giving up. My research is done, *thanks* to Grace. I let her take me away yesterday, and because I left an experiment alone, rather than hovering over it, the thing produced."

"Splendid!" Mrs. Cabilla clapped her hands. "I said you needed to—"

"Walk a mile in another's feet," *Abuelo* interrupted.

She flipped her hand in an airy gesture. "Yes, that. And it worked."

"Well, I solved the mystery. I know the secret. In a few more days I can finalize my preventative for paronychial infection."

"Where is Gracie?" Olaf interrupted.

"My question exactly," Dan said.

Everyone, at last, went silent.

"You don't know?" Em asked.

"I left her in my room."

"When we got here, your mother and father were all alone in the lab."

"Oh, no." Dan could imagine the scene he'd missed. His mother was queen of scenes. "I've got to find her. Where would she go?"

Panic set in. What if Grace disappeared and he never heard from her again? He'd only discovered the power of love, the amazing peace to be found in Grace's arms. He'd also just picked up a great, big package she needed to see.

"Her car is still here, bad man."

Dan raised an eyebrow at Olaf. "Do you think you could stop calling me that?"

"No."

Dan sighed. Olaf had let him live. Dan would let well enough alone.

Olaf was right. Grace's car was right where she had left it. He glanced at the woods. Where else could she be? He retrieved the package from his car, admonished everyone else to go home and mind their own business for at least a day, then he went in search of Grace.

Within a half an hour, he was lost. Actually, he'd been lost all of his life—until yesterday.

He'd be lost for the rest of his life, unless he found her, or she found him.

Dan found a tree, hugged the trunk, just for the hell of it, and sat down at the base to wait.

* * *

Grace stomped through the woods, cursing beneath her breath. She'd gone from devastated to downright furious. How could the same thing happen to the same person in the same lifetime?

Bad karma. That's what it was. No more men for her. Ever.

She'd given up Project Hope for him. At least for a few hours. Her walk to Mrs. Cabilla's had been a futile attempt to use exercise to make the urge to cry, and shriek, and kick someone abate. She'd planned to take the grant right back, but neither the woman, nor her minion, were anywhere to be found.

Now she had to walk back to Dan's and get her car. Sometimes she was just too dumb to live. She hoped Dan's wife, and her classy chauffeur, whom Grace had snarled at as she stomped toward the woods, were gone by now.

She should never have run off. She should have stayed right there and blasted Dan as soon as he showed up from wherever it was he'd slunk off to. One thing she'd learned from the Jared incident, closure was necessary. She had not had closure with Jared, and he'd haunted her for far too long.

She intended to have closure with Dan—right after she punched him in the nose.

"Help?"

Grace stopped, tilted her head and listened. "Anybody out there?"

Grace sighed. Another lost camper. While she was in no mood for search and rescue, she could not just walk off and leave someone alone. Even if she sent back the cavalry, the lost wanderer would no doubt have wandered off.

Grace followed the sound of the voice, which, oddly enough, didn't sound panicked, but it did sound familiar.

When she emerged into a clearing, she discovered why. Dan Chadwick was hugging a tree. He looked ridiculous.

"What are you doing?"

"What does it look like? I'm lost."

"You are not."

He let go of the tree. "I am. And I'll always be lost without you."

"Ah, go tell it to your wife."

"My who?"

"Penelope Chadwick."

"My mother?"

Grace gaped. "Your-your . . ."

"Mother. What did she say to you?"

"She looked too young to be your mother."

"I'm sure she'd be thrilled to hear that, as would her plastic surgeon. Happily, I'm no longer talking to my family, so I won't be able to pass along the compliment. Now why in hell would you think she was my wife?"

"It's happened before."

He looked confused. "You've met her before?"

"No, I've met the wife of the man I thought I loved, although last time I wasn't fresh out of his bed, but at my father's funeral."

Understanding dawned. "This would be the first man you slept with?"

"Bingo."

"Ah, baby, I'm sorry. He's pond scum, but I'm not. I promise. What did my mother say to make those eyes look so sad?"

Grace was having a hard time getting her mind around Dan calling her 'baby' without sounding silly, before she moved on to the fact that Dan's wife was actually his mother. Or rather he didn't have a wife, but he did have a mother. Whom he wasn't talking to. Grace had jumped to a whopper of a conclusion.

Dan suddenly snapped his fingers in front of her face. "Grace? Stay with me here. What did she say to upset you?"

"That I was your latest rebellion. You do this a lot, Dan?"

"Fall in love? Never."

"Love?" Grace couldn't seem to stop repeating him like an idiot.

"I meant to tell you this morning. I meant to tell you a lot of things. Like how I'm lost without you. How I want to marry you." He held out a manila envelope. "And I wanted to show you this."

Warily she took the offering, tore open the package and skimmed the contents. "What is it?"

"It's a report on Project Hope. I gathered all the available data on stress relief in children, put it together in a scientific manner, and sent the information out to all the stiffs I knew. You can see by the letters, I think there are about fifty so far, that you're on your way."

"But—why?"

"Your project is deserving, you just weren't presenting it in a language these guys could understand. I speak their language in my sleep."

"Why would you do that for me? You need the money."

"No, I don't."

"I told Mrs. Cabilla to give you the grant."

"And I told her to give it right back to you."

"Quit being stubborn, Dan, your work is everything to you. I saw you crying in the lab last night. I couldn't bear to make you so sad."

"I wasn't crying. I was laughing."

"Laughing? What could possibly be funny? Your life's work is ruined."

"No, my life's work is done. Because you made me forget time and live a little, the answer became clear."

"I thought your experiment was crap."

"Very interesting crap it turns out. Marry me?"

"So you can commit the ultimate rebellion?"

"Maybe." He wiggled his eyebrows. "Come on, Grace, be rebellious for the rest of your life. Marry me."

"Why? To annoy your parents?"

"Although that's always fun, I don't think it's worth getting married over."

Shadows from the trees danced across his face, making his eyes very hard to read, but his grin told the tale.

"You're serious."

"Very. You showed me your world, Grace, and it's beautiful. I don't want to be lost without you. I don't want to be lost ever again. You told me once when you wish on a star, your dreams come true. Make my dream come true. Be my partner, Grace, in life and in Project Hope."

She looked deep in her heart and saw the truth. Without him, she'd be hugging trees for the rest of her life, too.

"Marry me." He held out his hand. "Let me hold you every night. Let me help you every day."

Grace smiled and put her hand in his. "You know what, Doc? That's just what I had in mind."

Epilogue

One year later

"Yoo-hoo." Em's voice drifted throughout the lower level of the house on Elm Street. "It's time."

Dan slapped the last bit of tape on a box of blankies going to St. Cecilia's Children's Hospital. Next he would check his e-mail for the week's website donations. Project Hope had taken off with such force, their first problem had been finding enough blankets to go around.

"Time for what?" he called absently.

He'd enlisted the help of area nursing homes and summer day camps, asking them to make quilts and afghans as their art projects. The response was a flood.

The job he'd taken, teaching premed courses at a nearby college, put his medical training to use, and Dan discovered he was pretty good with bright young minds.

"Time for what, do you think?" Em snapped from the entryway. "For a doctor, you are so dense."

Em left the room, and for a minute, Dan kept working. The zone was the zone, whether it be research science or blankie delivery. But the commotion in the foyer penetrated at last.

"I will carry Gracie up the stairs."

"Olaf, I can walk just fine."

"And drop the baby out upon her head?"

"I doubt things will happen quite that fast."

"Grace!" Dan jumped up and ran into the hall. Grace, huge and happy with their first child, smiled indulgently.

The Jewels and Olaf shook their heads. Dan and Olaf had worked out a peaceable coexistence because of their love for Grace, though Olaf still hissed at him once in awhile. Because Dan understood why, he let him.

"It's too early," he said.

"Tell that to Junior." Grace continued her journey toward the third floor of the house, where it seemed everyone was going.

"Hey, there are hospitals for this, you know?"

"I know. Isn't it awful? What could be more natural than to bring your child into the world right in your very own home?"

They'd been having the same argument for eight months now. As usual, Grace agreed with everything he said, and Dan kept losing, but he'd vowed to keep trying until the bitter end. "And they have doctors who specialize in delivering babies."

She kept right on climbing. "You're a doctor."

He followed and lifted her into his arms. "I'm not that kind of doctor."

She gave him her amazing Grace smile. "You always say that."

"It's always true."

Dear Reader:

I hope you enjoyed WHEN YOU WISH. Grace and Dan had me laughing from the day they marched into my mind. The Jewels and Olaf were good for a chuckle or two, as well. I've spent quite a bit of time in northern Wisconsin, and I've always wanted to set a novel there. WHEN YOU WISH cried out for just such a setting.

My next novel for Kensington will be the first book in the ROCK CREEK SERIES, part of Kensington's new line of connected historical romances titled Ballad. If you liked the Magnificent Seven, you'll love the guys who come to Rock Creek, Texas. Look for the series to begin in 2001.

I love to hear from readers. If you would like a bookmark, please send an SASE to:

Lori Handeland
P.O. Box 736
Thiensville, WI 53092

For an up-to-date schedule of my novels and my backlist titles, check out my Web site at: http://www.eclectics.com/lorihandeland

BOOK YOUR PLACE ON OUR WEBSITE AND MAKE THE READING CONNECTION!

We've created a customized website just for our very special readers, where you can get the inside scoop on everything that's going on with Zebra, Pinnacle and Kensington books.

When you come online, you'll have the exciting opportunity to:

- View covers of upcoming books

- Read sample chapters

- Learn about our future publishing schedule (listed by publication month *and author*)

- Find out when your favorite authors will be visiting a city near you

- Search for and order backlist books from our online catalog

- Check out author bios and background information

- Send e-mail to your favorite authors

- Meet the Kensington staff online

- Join us in weekly chats with authors, readers and other guests

- Get writing guidelines

- AND MUCH MORE!

**Visit our website at
http://www.zebrabooks.com**

COMING IN DECEMBER FROM
Zebra Bouquet Romances

#73 TAMING BEN, by Colleen Faulkner
___(0-8217-6733-X $4.99US/$6.99CAN)

Ben Gordon is dead set against long-term relationships. But when he meets Mackenzie Sayer, he can't forget her. And it feels like they've met before.... Mackenzie can't believe Ben doesn't remember her from high school ... *she* remembers *him!* And when their volatile professional interaction turns into a very sensual personal reaction, she can't stay away. Maybe this time ...

#74 SOLITARY MAN, by Karen Drogin
___(0-8217-6734-8 $4.99US/$6.99CAN)

Rugged cop Kevin Manning had promised to care for his murdered partner's sister. But when comforting her leads to a night of passion, he leaves, sure he has nothing to offer. Months later he returns, to find her carrying his child. She can't forgive him for abandoning her. Still, something in his gaze tells her he needs her as much as she needs him....

#75 HEARTS AT RISK, by Suzanne Barrett
___(0-8217-6735-6 $4.99US/$6.99CAN)

Forced out of his lucrative start-up company, Tom McKittrick retires to his family estate and cancels the long-term lease on his caretaker's cottage. But the charming, reclusive woman who lives there is not about to let him order her out of her cozy retreat. She just has to teach this hunky guy to relax ... sow the seeds of romance ... and let nature take its course....

#76 THE LITTLEST MATCHMAKER, by Laura Phillips
___(0-8217-6736-4 $4.99US/$6.99CAN)

Lindsey Latimer wants Justine Shaw to marry her daddy, tycoon Kane Latimer. Justine soon learns Kane can easily destroy her hard-won career, yet he *still* makes her forget he's the last man she'd ever wed! Kane is well aware of Justine's charms. But he's decided a new mother for Lindsay will be *everything* Justine *isn't*. Meanwhile, he'll resist everything she is—beautiful, talented, perfect for him.

Call toll free **1-888-345-BOOK** to order by phone or use this coupon to order by mail. *ALL BOOKS AVAILABLE 12/05/00.*

Name _____

Address _____

City _____ State _____ Zip_____

Please send me the books I have checked above.

I am enclosing $_____
Plus postage and handling* $_____
Sales tax (in NY and TN) $_____
Total amount enclosed $_____

*Add $2.50 for the first book and $.50 for each additional book.

Send check or money order (no cash or CODs) to:

Kensington Publishing Corp., Dept. C.O., 850 Third Avenue, NY, NY 10022

Prices and numbers subject to change without notice. Valid only in the U.S.

All orders subject to availability.

Visit our website at **www.kensingtonbooks.com**.

Put a Little Romance in Your Life With
Fern Michaels

__Dear Emily	0-8217-5676-1	$6.99US/$8.50CAN
__Sara's Song	0-8217-5856-X	$6.99US/$8.50CAN
__Wish List	0-8217-5228-6	$6.99US/$7.99CAN
__Vegas Rich	0-8217-5594-3	$6.99US/$8.50CAN
__Vegas Heat	0-8217-5758-X	$6.99US/$8.50CAN
__Vegas Sunrise	1-55817-5983-3	$6.99US/$8.50CAN
__Whitefire	0-8217-5638-9	$6.99US/$8.50CAN